WITH A LITTLE HELP

HENK SLUIS

WITH A LITTLE HELP

HENK SLUIS

HENK SLUIS

ALSO, BY HENK SLUIS

POPPIES FOR THE DEAD

THE VEGETABLE GARDEN
(WITH LISA GONZALES)

WITH A LITTLE HELP

June 8, 2025

© June 8, 2025 Authored by Henk B. Sluis
h3sluis@gmail.com

Library and Archives Canada Cataloguing in Publication

Registered in Canada.

eBook Publishing

ISBN 978-1-0689331-3-4

HENK SLUIS

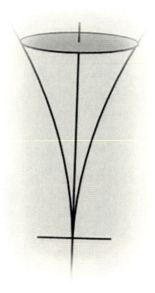

eBook Publishing

DEDICATED TO

LINDA SLUIS

MY LOVE FOR YOU IS FOREVER

Ink

Ink spills like fire on weary skin,
A blade of truth pressed deep within.
Each stroke defies the empire's hold,
A silent war in black and gold.

Names unmasked in crimson hue,
Etched in flesh where scars accrue.
Not just art, but wounds that speak,
A reckoning carved in lines so bleak.

Ink burns where justice fades,
Silent screams beneath the blades.
Each needle strikes, each shadow bleeds,
A reckoning for corporate greed.

Their wealth was built on stolen land,
Their empire raised by broken hands.
But skin remembers, ink speaks loud—
A revolution wrapped in shrouds.

unknown

X

WITH A LITTLE HELP

TABLE OF CONTENT

HENK SLUIS

WITH A LITTLE HELP

Chapter 1

"You know, Mabelle has this pitch in her voice, the one that tells you that you're stepping on broken glass." You're wearing shoes so it doesn't hurt, yet. But it's a clear warning."

May has been looking out of the car's window. It's past midnight with light rain making it hard to see. She has been listening to her partner's latest outing with Mabelle. How he ended up with her boggles the mind. She turns to look at him, her eyes roll in her head and it reminds him of the times he played dice, two black dots on a bone white background. Snake eyes.

"What?"

"Turn around, let's circle the block."

Sargeant Miles Staples slows down and does a U-turn, after two years as her training officer, he is familiar with that tone, her radar is up to full power. He imagines a green dot on the screen, the ping, ping, ping, as it scans the area, the sound keeping in time with the wipers as it sweeps the drizzle from the windshield. They circle an old, abandoned brick building, the remnants of a bygone automobile industry, its windows long since smashed out leaving large openings that once held glass every 20 feet, just the hollow shell remains. Two stories, a half block long surrounded by a hurricane fence which lays flat in more areas than are standing.

She rolls down the window. "There, main level southwest corner, a light is moving around."

Miles turns off the headlights and rolls the cruiser another 50 yards before coming to a stop. "Call it in, let's ask for some backup."

"Unit 319 requesting backup at Brush Street and Piquette." Two minutes go by before a static response from dispatch that unit 140 is in route.

May asks for dispatch to repeat the last.

Miles responds, "Pretty hard to believe that in this day and age we can't get a decent communications system!"

They wait in silence for a few minutes and Miles opens the door, "Ok let's have a look see, probably a guy getting lucky." He pulls the shotgun from the rack before getting out. "You go around the outside, I'll go through the inside. Let's stay parallel with each other."

May moves along the brick wall slowly peering into each opening and making sure she can see that Miles isn't getting ahead of her, or her ahead of him. She ducks under each opening so she can't be spotted from the inside.

Miles moves slowly. It's black except for the dim glow every 20 yards or so coming from the streetlights drifting through the openings. He stops to turn on his own flashlight but hesitates when he hears voices. He ducks behind an empty 55-gallon drum.

Miles overhears, "You don't have to choose, tell you what, I'll throw in a box of nine mill for the Luger and 38's for the Smith and Wesson and close the deal for an even thousand."

May approaches the next window and sees Miles has taken cover. She sees two figures in the low light of a lantern standing on a stack of pallets high enough to form a makeshift table. On it are what looks like four handguns.

Miles waves May forward and she moves towards the next window. She draws her weapon and checks to see if the safety is off. She has only fired her weapon on the range, and never with just one hand.

Miles steps up and as he does a rat squeals as it comes running from behind the drum, the voices stop mid sentence, and the light turns off. A shot rings out. May finds herself against a brick wall between the two windows. She hesitates for a split second, move to the next window or turn back to the last window. She chooses the former and hopes it will position her behind the suspects. It takes her five seconds to reach the next window. She spots one of the suspects at a full run towards the far side of the building. She sweeps her pistol and the heavy flashlight to the right and sees the second suspect standing over Miles who is laying beside the barrel, with his hands stretched out before him in an attempt to block the next round. In the spotlight May can make out a man in dark clothing about ten yards away.

He has a revolver pointed at Miles's head. She hears him say "I'm not going back."

Miles yells "No don't!" May raises her weapon to the shooting position as she was instructed during her training and as she has practiced so many times on the range, but it feels awkward, not having two hands on the gun. Without hesitation she fires four shots at the suspect. She sees the impact that the .40 caliber round fired from a Glock 23 can make. It is certainly not the same as the paper targets she was using for practice. The sound strikes her eardrums, again, not the same as on the range where she always wears ear protection. The suspect's body shudders three times before falling face down on the concrete floor. May swings around to her left to see that the second suspect is long gone. Three weapons still lay on the makeshift table. She climbs through the window opening keeping her gun on the man lying motionless on the floor. She moves quickly but stays low as she approaches the man only three feet from Miles. She gives him a solid kick in the side. He remains motionless. She holsters her weapon.

"Are you alright?"

"Fuck no, I've been shot."

She sees blood spreading from a hole in his shirt just below his right-side ribcage. She takes off her raincoat, balls it up and puts it over the hole, applying pressure. Miles screams in pain. She grabs her mike and calls dispatch "Unit 319 Code 10-33 we need backup and ambulance at Brush Steet and Piquette, we have an officer down with gunshot. Be on the lookout for a male

suspect in dark clothing running Southwest from this location."
She looks at Miles, "How are you doing?"

"Son of a bitch shot me in the same place I got hit five years ago.
Why don't they make these jackets longer!"

She gives him a little smile "I'll go get the first aid kit."

"Not before you cuff this bag of shit!"

"Why? He sure looks dead."

"Because it's procedure and this is going to be all over the
media. That means lots of brass, internal affairs and the review
board will be looking at us through a microscope. We are going
to do this by the book."

May takes out her handcuffs and cuffs the suspect.

"Now, do you feel safe enough that I can go and get the kit before
you bleed out?"

She is surprised when he replies with a firm "NO, you don't seem
to realize how big a deal this is. We are in for a shit storm, find
the gun, I don't see it anywhere."

She pulls out her flashlight and scans the surrounding area.
Miles tries to sit up but quickly lays back down with a grunt.

"Stay put, I'll find it." She lifts up the barrel that Miles was hiding
behind. It had tipped over when he was shot. Even though it was
empty it still weighted nearly fifty pounds, she moved it with
ease.

"I don't see it. It's got to be here, we both saw it, I'm sure the forensics team will find it."

"You bet I saw it; he was five feet from me pointing it in my face." He lets out a sigh, frustration and worry showed on his face, he knows what's coming. "We are not going to leave this for them to find, it's too important."

May stops her search and looks up, it just hit her that she has killed someone. She stands motionless as the vision of the man's body jerks in slow motion with the impact of each shell. She looks at Miles and sees the concern on his face. What should she do, she seems to be frozen with a thousand thoughts, none of which result in a plan. In the recesses of her mind a voice she has heard before speaks out *"snap out of it, look under the body."* It's her instincts kicking in, they have never let her down before, so she grabs the man's arm and rolls him over.

She looks at Miles and sees that he has his eyes shut. "Got it."

He opens his eyes "Ok, good, kick it out here so it's visible and check his vitals, it'll look good on the report."

She does so, checking for a pulse on his neck, trying not to get blood all over herself in the process.

"Can I go now, and get the kit before you bleed out?"

The sound of multiple sirens can be heard in the distance. They bounce off the walls making it hard to tell which direction they are coming from. She takes off at a slow run but only gets halfway to the patrol car before stopping to toss her lunch.

Chapter 2

"Hi, can you tell me where I can find Sergeant Miles Staples?" The receptionist taps on the computer keyboard, "he's in room 429, that's the general ward, the elevators are on your left." She points in the general direction and goes back to typing on her cellphone. May thinks she's too young to be out of school but it's a brave new world.

May approaches the door to room 429 and sees it's open. She steps in and sees Miles sitting up in his bed. He has a smile on his face.

"Well, if it isn't Miss Mawusi Jane Sheppard. You know, white lilies are for funerals."

She looks down at the bundle of flowers she purchased in the lobby, then glances around the room. There isn't a spot remaining that isn't occupied with flowers.

"You didn't tell me your mother owned a florist shop."

"Funny. What took you so long, every member of the precinct has dropped by."

"You must have told them you had donuts." She walks around the room picking up get well cards. There had to be at least 50, with some big name signatures. She comes to the bedside, "How are you feeling?"

He looks up at her, she is just over six feet tall, dark skinned with broad shoulders. Her hair is in cornrows and falls down her back. She had played basketball and it was her ticket to a full scholarship via University of Mercy, but it was a means to an end.

"Ok, not my first rodeo. Thanks for, you know....saving my life."

May says, "No big deal." She looks in his eyes and sees they are starting to fill with tears. He turns his head away and pretends to reach for the glass of water.

 "Are you giving the nurses a hard time? There was one at least sixty that could be a match for you."

Miles is actually forty-nine years old and will soon be able to retire, but he loves his job. He has no family, not even a cat. At times May feels sorry for her partner and on occasion has tried to fix him up with a companion. They quickly grew close and trust each other, to the point where now he will even let her drive.

May says, "Do you remember the lady from the car accident on Bishop and Wilkes?"

"The car accident? Mrs. Stuart? That happened two weeks ago, what about her?"

"She called me yesterday and wanted to know how the investigation was going. She asked if there was anything she should do if she was going to be called to testify. She's afraid she's going to be sued."

"Sued? She was a witness to a traffic accident. How did she know to call you? I was the one that gave her my card."

"I don't know, and it's 'Miss' by the way, I think she has some connection within the department because she seemed to know a bit about us, so I ran her plates. They are registered to a Bentley. Her driver's licence has a swanky Sherwood Park address."

"Hey, we handled that call like any other, by the book. It was a minor fender bender, that guy was faking the neck injury, and he was getting mouthy with her. I just told him to back off and stop intimidating a potential witness. But we still called the ambulance just like he asked."

"The knight in shining armour. She was just following up as a concerned citizen. Diane, that's her name. She did ask if you were married."

"And you told her what?"

"Like I said, she has connections, I don't want to piss off the powers that be."

"What year was the Bentley?"

With a smile May says, "Brand spanking new, still got temporary plates. Do you want to call her or do a drive by and give her an update? Just, you know, to close the loop."

She walks back to a table that has the flowers and cards, picks one up and hands it to him. It has letterpress printing, embossing, and foil stamping using traditional Florentine artisan techniques, it screams money and is signed Miss Diane Stuart.

Miles raises his left eyebrow and hands the card back to her. "How was the interview with the review board?"

"You were dead right, I had no idea the shit storm this would raise. The guy had a rap sheet longer than a roll of toilet paper, served six years for assault. But they treated me like I was the bad guy, wouldn't give me any feedback on the results of the inquiry."

"They just left here, put me through the same thing but I knew one of them from the last time I got shot. His name is Briggs and he told me, off the record, it was a clean shoot. We're in the clear."

May gives a sigh of relief, "Captain Masters called me in and told me that I would be working a desk for a while. Said I had to go see a shrink, a Dr. Malinda Salsburg. Apparently, it's policy after a traumatic event. How did you end up getting shot before? I wish I had known you would be a bullet magnet!"

"It was five years ago, serving a warrant. We knocked on the door and a round came straight through and hit me just below the vest. By the way, she's not a shrink, she's a psychologist and has her own practice on Bolder Street but does a lot of work for the Emergency Service. Hey, maybe we can do a joint session and save the department a few bucks. I would like to know some of your most intimate thoughts."

May rolls her eyes "that would be the end of me."

Chapter 3

The morning coffee just doesn't taste the same, she thinks about what it was but can't put her finger on it, more... bitter. Or, let's be honest, would it be what you heard on the news is affecting your perception? Robert Williams was his name; she hadn't known that until now. It had been three days since the shooting. She hadn't even checked to see if he had any ID on him at the time. Jesus, what type of cop does that! Now they where telling the world he was twenty-eight and had a four-year-old son. She wonders if there was a mother in the picture.

The review board had been brutal. Sitting around here for the last three days wasn't helping. It felt good to put the uniform back on and get back to the precinct even if it was desk duty until the official report came out and she had completed her sessions with this Dr. Salsburg. She wondered what it would be like. "I guess I'll find out tomorrow."

As May goes through the front door she is met by Captain Master, "Welcome back. Before roll call, Commander Williams wants to see you in the briefing room. Afterwards we'll get you set up at a desk and talk more. She goes to the bathroom and checks herself in the mirror. She has only met the two stars once and feels apprehensive about the meeting.

She walks down the hall and sees that the break room door is open. He is at the counter pouring himself a coffee and as she walks in, he turns and smiles. A roar, accompanied with clapping and shouts break out from both sides of the room, most of the precinct has squeezed in to welcome her back. She is overwhelmed with the response. Williams is clapping and moves forward to shake her hand. "Everyone just wanted to thank you and tell you what a great job you did. The whole division is proud of the way you handled yourself."

"Wow, thanks guys, you sure made it easier to come back. I must say I was a little nervous about the reception."

Master comes up behind her, she hadn't noticed him when he had slipped into the room. "I don't know what to say, I'm so embarrassed."

"You did fine. Come with me, lets put that college degree to work."

Chapter 4

It's not much but it has her picture and a brief bio. May dims the screen; it's too bright on her eyes. Her second search using Linkedin gave better results than Google.

Dr. Malinda Salsburg, Psychologist.

She has a bachelor's degree in psychology from Stanford University. She took her Masters at the University of Michigan as well as her Doctorate. She also took Specialized Training in Trauma Psychology and completed her internship at the Rainbow Rehabilitation Center. She took her Examination for Professional Practice in Psychology (EPPP) and is licensed to practice in Michigan. She also sees that Dr. Salsburg is a Certified First Responder Treatment Provider (CFRP).

May scrolls back to the picture. Auburn hair that hasn't begged to see a stylist. Large, framed glasses and a smile that will light up any room. Her skin is light brown, not like her own which is dark, despite her mixed race. It's hard to judge how tall she is from the picture because it only shows her from the chest upwards, which is larger than hers. May wished she had bigger boobs. She is strikingly good looking and probably five years May's senior. Did she have the picture air brushed?

Why is she making comparisons to herself?

She had talked to Miles about the sessions and he said it was "no big deal, just tell her what she wants to hear. If you clam up, you'll be there forever." But the upcoming sessions still bothered her. What was she afraid of?

May thinks to herself, 'alright let's get this over with.' The appointment is for ten o'clock.

The majority of Dr. Salsburg's practice is with the Detroit Police Dept. but she is not an employee. Her office is a two-storey brownstone, a discreet distance from headquarters, which allows her to maintain her independence and provide a feeling of confidentiality for her clients. Her office is on the second floor, which she shares with a dental practice. The main floor is occupied by a medical supply store. The door is frosted with her name professionally stenciled on it in gold block letters. It opens to a small anti-room with four chairs and coffee table, but there is no desk or receptionist. She is faced with another door. A camera is mounted near the ceiling. A moment later the door opens, and Dr. Malinda Salsburg walks in wearing a four-hundred-dollar business suit and killer heels.

Not a good start.

She had chosen not to wear her uniform but had worn capri jeans and a sleeveless blouse. The tattoo of an African mask along with a spear is on her right leg just above her ankle. She always wears a necklace made from an elephant tusk that has the nsoromma image on it. It looks like an eclipsing star with eight points. The necklace is very old and has been passed down on the female side for generations.

An office it's not, no computer, no desk, no filing cabinet, no diploma on the wall, not even a window. It is more like a living room in an upscale home with wall-to-wall carpeting, not that industrial Berber, but thick plush Saxony that begs your feet to take your shoes off. Two comfortable chairs and a chaise lounge, (it was probably an upgrade for 'the couch') and a round coffee table made up the only furniture. There were a few pieces of art on the wall. All had the same frame but each were from a different artist and had different subject matter.

The room had high ceilings and there was a modern chandelier that gave off soft lighting. There was also additional lighting that came from two free standing floor lamps. There were two other doors, one, she assumed would be for a powder room and the other probably led to where the paperwork was done. The room met its objectives, which was to provide a relaxing, disarming setting.

"Welcome, why don't you sit down and make yourself comfortable. Before we start, let me assure you that whatever you say here is confidential and won't be repeated without your permission. My role is to make sure that your mental health is stable enough for you to return to active duty as a patrol officer. The only information forwarded to your supervisor is a yes or no to that question."

The room becomes quiet, for two minutes the clock over the door did a slow tick, tick, tick.

"Ok, I will tell you a story about my life, my family. and then you tell me one about yours, deal?" May nods her head in agreement.

"My whole family is strictly catholic. My younger sister is a nun, and my older brother is a bishop, soon to be a cardinal. Dad is very excited about this development and will tell anyone who will listen, how his son will one day lead the catholic church. He is very proud of them both.

"To his never-ending disappointment though, I have lapsed in my faith. Dear dad wants one thing more than even the ticket to heaven that he believes my siblings can earn him. He always gives me a lecture and a hard look at every opportunity, but I hold a trump card up my sleeve, and he knows it. One day I will steal the limelight from my perfect brother and sister. What do you think that is?"

May thinks for a moment "You're the only one that can give him grandchildren!"

They both break out in smiles and have a little chuckle.

"Ok, that is a good story, I don't think I can top it, but here goes. My father is Caucasian and works in law-enforcement, mom is an associate professor and a track coach. My grandmother, Felicia, immigrated from the Kingdom of Dahomey in West Africa when she was just a child.

"I have a very strong bond with my grandmother who has a direct ancestral line back to the shaman for Tegbesu. Her mother, my great-grandmother, would tell her enchanting stories of her life in the village where she lived. Stories like the one about her spirit animals that would come in the night and lay beside her to keep her warm and protect her. How, when she was lost in the forest, a tribesman came wearing a wooden mask and a hawk on his shoulder told her how to find her way home. He said, "follow my bird and it will lead you to your village."

"When she told the story to her father, he suspected that the plants she had been eating was Tabernanthe iboga a hallucinogenic plant, the elders in the village believed otherwise."

"And what do you think?"

"I think it may have encouraged her to draw on some of the old mythical stories that circulated from the days of the witch doctors."

Chapter 5

May's grandmother says, "It belonged to my mother, your great grandmother. She never took it off, she always believed it was a good luck charm, some kind of talisman. But to be honest, my fingers got too fat, so I stopped wearing it a few years ago. Before she died she made me promise to keep it on the female side of the family. It has been passed down for over eight generations, you could consider it to be a birthday present from her."

May holds the ring in her left hand, it was heavy and looked small in diameter but was quite wide. She had met her great-grandmother once ten years ago on her first trip to Africa. She had a similar build and wondered how it had fit on her fingers. It had African symbols carved on both the inside and outside, dark in color and held four small, imbedded stones each a different color, a green, a blue, a white and a red. She slipped it on her right ring finger. Surprisingly, it felt comfortable, like it belonged.

"I love it, it's the best birthday gift I could think of."

"You're welcome, but its actually from your great grandmother. My gift to you is in the great room, and we had better get back, your guests will be wondering where you are."

They made their way from the office to the great room. As they came down the spiral stairs the gathering of friends and family turned and began clapping. "Happy birthday" rang out in unison. Glasses were raised and the crowd of forty or more moved forward to hug and kiss her.

May spotted Mabelle at the bar with Miles who had fully recovered. May was not surprised that he had brought Mabelle as his date. They had been seeing each other on an occasional basis. She was holding on to his arm like a boa constrictor. Each had a martini. May asked one of the bartenders for a gin and tonic, which he quickly filled. There was something about Mabelle that May did not like. She believed Miles could do better. May had hoped that he would have the nerve to follow up with Diane Stuart. She had been hopeful when they had visited the garage where the accident had occurred and obtained a copy of the video showing the event. He had downloaded it to his phone and reviewed it in the squad car. It was obvious that Diane was not involved and only acted as a witness. As it turned out, Diane Stuart did have connections with the DPD, she was on the standing committee for the Detroit Police Officer Association (DPOA).

Miles scanned the room like a burglar sizing up his next job. The space was vast, reminiscent of a cavern, with ceilings soaring twenty feet high. The marble floor, adorned with an intricate map of the solar system, reflected the grandeur of the house. A string quartet played softly on a small stage, surrounded by several large pieces of African art. In the center, a large console table boasted a four-tiered floral arrangement, overlooking a selection of party foods like a sentinel daring anyone to disturb the arrangement. Waiters in white tuxedos circled the room, offering trays of hors d'oeuvres.

Malinda approaches May and gives her a hug. "You've been holding out on me. This is one hell of a place; I had no idea you were part of royalty."

May smiles, "It's not mine silly, it's my grandmother's, but I suppose it will be mine one day. My great grandmother was almost royalty, she was the adviser to the tribal king. In two thousand, diamonds were discovered on our land and it made her very wealthy. Mom has no interest in this place. She would tear it all down and turn it into a physics lab. I love it though. It brings me closer to my heritage. Would you like a quick look around?

The tour ended in the library, which was almost the size of the great room. It was spectacular, row after row of books, with an extensive section exclusively on African culture and history. Any area that did not have bookshelves was covered in African art, a full-size wood carving of a tribesman stood in the center of the room. Fishing and hunting spears were displayed on the wall along with wooden face masks, some adorned with colorful feathers. A display case held an uncut diamond the size of a fist.

May's grandmother walks in and says, "No, it's a replica of the one found on the property. May, your other guests are asking about you." She turned and with the wave of her arm, the troops followed.

Chapter 6

"Let's go back to the night of the shooting."

"Malinda, I don't know what more I can tell you about it, I have been over it so many times with you." May shows a little frustration, she wants the whole thing over with. It's been three months, and the review board still hasn't released their report. Everyone said it was a clean shoot, so what is taking so long?

"You never told me why you had Sergeant Staples circle the block. You mentioned that you didn't see any lights on in the building, so what triggered the alert?"

May feels uncomfortable answering the question, she doesn't know why. Dr. Salsburg notices she twists the ring on her finger in contemplation.

After a long moment May exhales, "I can't put my finger on it... exactly. I guess it was just another feeling that I had. A shadow seems to come over me, like a chill running up my spine. I mean, everybody you talk to has some variation of it, premonition, a hunch, intuition, but mine somehow seems different."

"How often do you get these feelings? Is there anything that you can think of that might trigger them?"

May takes a moment to think about it, "It's been getting stronger. I have learned to trust it more." She pauses for a moment. "You know, from when I first started as a DPD trainee, I have had thoughts, would I be able to take a life, but when I had to do it, well, it was like swatting a bug...that came out wrong. I didn't think of him as a bug, its just the reaction I had, it was just instinct, you do it.

May is tired and suggests, "Let's call this session over and go for coffee. You talked about that boutique you wanted to check out on Livernois."

"Ok, I don't have any other appointments so that sounds like a great idea. But there is something I want you to think about. Sometime in the future, would you be willing to go under hypnosis?"

"Can you do that? I would like to try it!"

Chapter 7

They had agreed to a small restaurant well known for its Asian cuisine located conveniently between the University and the precinct. May arrived just before the lunch rush hour. Her mother had a meeting with a doctoral student whom she was mentoring just after lunch, and she wanted time to prepare.

Between bits of sweet and sour pork her mother asks, "When do you think you'll be permitted back on patrol?"

"Oh, God, I hope its soon, I'm so bored pushing paper and filling out reports. I keep asking Captain Masters that same question, but his response is always the same. 'It's out of my hands, enjoy your 'easy time'. Take a page out of your partner's playbook." May can envision Masters looking over at Miles's temporary workstation and sees that he's sitting with his legs on the lower desk drawer, has a coffee cup in one hand and a magazine in the other.

"Well, I can't say that I look forward to you getting back on the street. The best Christmas present your father ever gave me was when he hung up the gun belt and took a desk job."

She notices the ring on May's finger, "Isn't that your great grandmother's ring?"

"It is. Grandma told me that before she passed it to you, it was passed to her by her mother, and that she got it from hers, and so on. Apparently, it originated with an ancestral medicine woman eight generations back. Where it came from and who made it has been lost to time. What do you think about the stories she tells?"

"It's a lot of mumbo jumbo, don't believe a word of it."

Chapter 8

"At the conclusion of our last session you talked about how you felt disassociated from the time that you saw the suspect running away. Can you clarify that further?

May looks at the ceiling and then lowers her gaze to Dr. Salsburg. "I really don't know how to describe it. I was scared shitless when I stood up and looked through the opening, expecting to take a round. Then immediately, like someone turned on a switch, I felt that I split into two parts. The fear had stepped back and the warrior stepped forward. I'm totally calm, it's a movie that I have seen played out a hundred times. I know what to do and how it will end. I see the first guy running for the far side of the building, I know exactly what to do. There are three guns remaining on the crates, so, he is not the immediate threat. I focus on the second guy; he must have the missing gun. I swing my Glock from left to right and spot him with his gun pointing down at Miles. He is telling him that he is not going back. Translated in my brain as 'I'm going to kill you'. My total focus is on keeping the gun steady and squeezing the trigger."

"You say it was like a warrior stepped forward, why?"

"I felt like I had become a different person, that it's not me. This person is cold and ruthless. I became someone without a conscience. She scares me, what if she comes out again?"

"Because you are aware how dangerous situations like these are, makes you a good cop. Your survival instincts kept you and your partner alive."

Chapter 9

Miles walks up to May's desk, she is compiling burglary statistics and creating a power point presentation to be presented by Commander Williams to the police commission tomorrow morning. The graph is heading in the right direction so the Commander should be in a good mood.

Miles is holding a coffee cup in his hand and passes it to May. "My source in Internal Affairs, Briggs, just told me they found the buyer in our shooting case. Apparently, they have had him under wraps for the last three days. The deal is, he gets a pass on all charges if he signs off on our statements."

Before May can respond, Captain Robert Masters, steps out of his office and signals them to come in. There are two chairs across from his desk but neither officer takes a seat.

"I just got the report back from IA and you have both been cleared of the shooting. Therefore, I can now 'officially' congratulate you on a job well done. The psychologist's report also came back with a clean bill of health. So, no need for any more sessions with Dr. Salsburg. You can clean up what you're doing, in your case Miles, that would be finishing your magazine article and be back on the streets tomorrow morning."

Chapter 10

She doesn't know if Miles has been avoiding it for her sake or his own, but they have been on patrol now for three days and have not gone anywhere near Brush Street and Piquette. She is about to broach the subject when a report comes over the radio. "Unit 319, report to Detective Mat Strouse at Howard and West Lafayette. Help secure a crime scene."

Miles turns on the blues and twos "there goes lunch."

They pull up to the crowded street corner and spot Detective Strouse giving instructions to two other patrol officers. "Hey Miles, good to see you back on the street. You must be officer Mawusi Sheppard, nice piece of work taking the trash out."

"Please, call me May and thank you." She has been warned by Captain Masters to expect this type of greeting and that the best response is to let it pass.

Strauss informs the team of a fresh triple homicide in the building, adding the chilling detail that the blood still glistens wet. He doesn't have any suspects yet. Miles sends May back to the unit to retrieve the crime scene tape. As she walks back her eyes catch sight of a blue commercial garbage dumpster in an alley, an instinctive alarm goes off within her. Against her better judgment, she decides to deviate from her mission and instead moves to the dumpster to investigate.

Just five yards from the dumpster, a girl bursts out from behind it like a startled rabbit and dashes down the alley. May shouts a warning, launching into pursuit with the agility of a sprinter. In a heartbeat, she tackles the fleeing girl, pinning her to the ground with determined force. She swiftly cuffs the girl's hands behind her back, demanding, "Why did you run? I just want to ask you a few questions." The girl's eyes dart nervously as she struggles to catch her breath. May notices a stain on her sweatshirt, it could be blood.

"Let's you and I have a chat with Detective Strouse shall we." As she begins walking down the alley, her head snaps to the dumpster, it seems involuntarily. She stops and turns the girl around and walks back to it. Looking between the wall and the dumpster, she sees a red backpack. In it, there are ten small packages containing a white powder along with a tenth-grade schoolbook on biology. "This wouldn't be yours by any chance?"

May calls her partner on the radio and gives him an update.

"Well, lookie here, only three days back on patrol and you solve a triple homicide. Nice work. Put her in the back of the unit and I'll inform Strouse that you solved his case."

"Very funny Miles, she looks barely fifteen years old. I doubt that she was able to take on three men, but she is scared as hell and may have seen something."

Chapter 11

"All right people settle down, this is a morning briefing, not a union meeting." Captain Masters pauses for a second and continues. "A boy has gone missing; he is eleven years old and is autistic. Adam Tilling was last seen at his school eleven hours ago. Someone really dropped the ball on this one. We are going to clean it up." Taking a laser pointer, he circles a five-block area on a map projected on the screen behind him. "Units 450, 313, 140, 251 and 319 will search this area on foot, the remaining units will search by car around the outside of this area extending outward. There are sheets with his picture and profile at the door. That's it, hit the streets."

Miles and May had been assigned to search a three-story apartment block. Their plan was to start on the roof and work their way down to the basement. They had engaged the landlord and the caretaker in the process to facilitate access to areas that could be locked. They would also be helpful as translators since many residents were from Malasia and didn't speak English. They could also help with the interviews as many would be suspicious of the police.

Every common area was opened and thoroughly checked. Garbage shoots, electrical rooms, storage rooms were all opened. Once done, they went to every apartment and interviewed the residents, making them aware of the lost boy.

On the second floor Miles knocked on B2 but received no response.

Mr. Aziz, the caretaker, explains that it was the residence of Mrs. Rahim. She didn't speak English and was seldom seen. She was in mourning as she had recently lost her husband and son in a motor vehicle accident. Miles checked the door, testing to see if it was locked. It was. May slipped an information sheet under the door. They proceeded down the hall, checking with each resident. As they approached F2 May slowed, she turned and spoke to Mr. Aziz, "How old was Mrs. Rahim's son?"

"He just had his tenth birthday party."

"Miles, lets go back to B2, I want to try again."

"We got a lot of ground to cover May, there was no one home or like he said, pointing to Aziz, she wants to be left alone because she's mourning."

"I just have this really strong feeling." With determination, she moves back to B2 and knocks loudly on the door with her fist. "Mrs. Rahim, this is the police, open the door." There is no response. She instinctively places her ear against the door. She instructs the caretake to use his key to open it.

"Hold on a minute, we don't have probable cause here May".

"I'm sure I heard a small voice; we have to check it out."

Miles knows his partner, and this is bullshit, there is something else at work here, but goes along with it anyway. "Is this another one of your hunches? You know the last one almost got me killed. God, I hope you're right, but before we do that, Mr. Aziz, do you know Mrs. Rahim?"

"Yes, I attended Mr. Rahim's and his son's funeral."

"Can you please knock on the door and call out to her for us please."

Mr. Aziz does so with a booming voice, with no results. Miles waits another moment, looks at May. "You still want to do this?" She thinks for a moment; *'he is in there'* and simply nods the affirmative. Miles orders the caretaker, "ok, unlock the door and step back please. Mrs. Rahim, this is the police, we are coming in." Miles has stepped back from the door; he doesn't want to be hit by a shotgun blast. He pushes the door open with his baton. Peering through the doorway, he sees a woman about thirty-five years old. She has on a yellow full-length dress with daisies imprinted on it. She is holding a rolling pin over her head with both hands. At the top of her voice, she screams in what Miles believes is Spanish, but he doesn't know for sure.

In the corner May spots a young boy, there is no question it is Adam.

Mr. Aziz turns to May "She says that she will protect her son with her life."

"Is there any chance she has more than one child?" asks May.

"No, I have known the family for three years, have had dinners with them. There are no other children."

Mrs. Rahim breaks down and slides to the floor. Her head is raised up to the heavens and she begins to cry. The sound of sorrow, so deep it freezes the group.

Miles slowly approaches her and takes the rolling pin from her lap where she had placed it. He gently lifts her up and puts her in hand cuffs.

The boy seems to be unhurt but makes no move or sound.

Miles tells May to call it in and to stay with the boy while he takes Mrs. Rahim to the car.

Chapter 12

Sargeant Miles Staples checks himself in the precinct bathroom mirror. He places his cap on his head and smiles, still pleased with how he looks in his dress uniform. Not bad for a guy just about to turn 50. He meets May in the lounge area. She's had her uniform tailored to fit her height. Her long black hair has been put up so that it's covered by her cap. Her forced smile did nothing to hide her nervousness. "You look great, should we go in?"

Miles leads the way to the briefing room; four chairs had been setup next to the podium. Captain Robert Masters sat next to Commander Williams, a two star, in command of Neighborhood East Bureau. Miles and May sat to their right. The room was filled to capacity. May spotted her father, who had flown in from Washington for the presentation ceremony. Her mother, and grandmother sat next to him. Dr. Salsburg and Diane Stuart where in the front row center next to Mr. and Mrs. Tilling. The rest of the audience was comprised of street officers, and civilian staff.

Commander Williams stood and approached the podium and made a speech, praising both Sargeant Miles Staples and May

(Mawusi) Jane Sheppard for their outstanding work in returning Adam Tilling to his parents unharmed. Captain Masters did the formal presentation of the Letter of Commendation, which was signed by the chief of police and the mayor. Official photographs were taken by the crime scene photographer and the media. It would probably make it to the next morning paper. It was all wrapped up within fifteen minutes.

May approached Commander Williams and asked what would happen to Mrs. Rahim.

"Well, after the assistant prosecutor explained the tragic circumstances that Mrs. Rahim had endured recently with the death of both her son and husband to Mr. and Mrs. Tilling, neither of them saw any benefit in prosecuting her. It would have been a different story if it hadn't been for your insightfulness and quick resolution in returning the boy."

"I don't know if you heard that young girl you apprehended with the cocaine, well, Detective Strouse found the same drugs at the crime scene. It turns out that she was a witness to the shooting. That was a nice piece of work on your part."

Chapter 13

Miles, in a casual tone says, "I think we have time to drop this off at Diane Stuart's residence." He holds up a USB drive. "Didn't you say she lives around here?"

May thinks, 'you've got to be kidding', but instead says, "Do you think I'm so stupid that I haven't figured out where we've been heading for the last 20 minutes? Was it by chance that you had a haircut yesterday, that you're wearing your best uniform, and your shoes are polished to a mirror? You have on enough aftershave to repel a skunk, and you want me to believe we are just in the vicinity to drop by?"

"It was your idea to go to the scene of the accident again and check to see if any of the establishments in the area had security video that could have recorded the event. See, that's why I think you'll make a great detective."

"You think that if you butter me up I'll back you on this little adventure. You are so seriously mistaken. We are way out of our patrol district and if dispatch wakes up and reports it, there will be questions."

Miles just turns to her and gives her his best smile. She loves it and points down the road "Tally Ho" is her only response.

They both had searched Diane's residence on Google Street View and so they were not surprised by its size. It had to be 5000 square feet on just the main level and was set on a two-acre lot surrounded by steel eight-foot-high security fence. They had to announce themselves via a call box which had a camera mounted on it before the gate swung open.

"I hope you told her we were coming by. A woman, especially one like her, doesn't like to receive her courtier without an opportunity to make herself presentable."

"Shit, do you think I messed up, I'll turn around and come back later."

"Big time but too late now, she's already seen you on the security system, just act cool. She is obviously into you. It's just a professional courtesy call, right?"

"Yeah, Yeah, right. Be cool." He says more to himself than to her.

The circular drive led them to the front of the house which had a large set of double wooden doors heavy enough to stop the castle siege. In front stands a nicely dressed man to greet them. He was tall, dark and handsome, about thirty years old.

"Good morning officers, is there something I can do for you?"

Miles speaks first, a Sargeant Staples and Officer Sheppard here to see Ms. Stuart regarding the incident on July 13th. We discovered some information that will be relevant to the case."

"Oh yes, she told me about it. Were you the officers at the scene? My name is Brandon; I take care of security and act as Ms. Stuart's driver. Please follow me." He leads them to what appears to be the library and shows them to a grouping of four chairs. "Diane is just finishing up a call and will be down shortly. Please make yourselves comfortable." He then leaves the room.

Miles plays with the thumb drive "This is stupid. What was I thinking, she's way out of my league. What do you think, Brandon her boy toy?"

"She didn't look to me to be interested in class, remember she sent you the flowers and a nice card. She obviously cares enough about you to do that."

Five long minutes pass before she enters the room. She appears to be in a very good mood, smiling and reaching out to shake their hands. "Brandon told me why you are here, thank you for coming. Please sit and tell me what your investigation discovered."

Miles tells her about the drive and that it proves she was only a witness and not involved in the accident.

"Thank you Sargeant Staples for taking the time to bring this to me. I have been a bit worried it would turn into something nasty. Could we take a look at the video using the computer in the office?"

"Certainly, and please call me Miles."

They followed her to the office which is bigger than the library, something suitable for the CEO of IBM. "Will you join me for coffee while we watch the video?" Before they could answer she presses a button under the desk and says "Brandon, can you please bring coffee for our guests? Brandon has been with me since he left the marines, and he's been a rock since my husband's murder seven years ago."

May scans the desk looking for a microphone but doesn't see anything resembling one.

Moments later, Brandon, walked in with a silver tray of coffee and an assortment of pastries. Bending down to set the tray, May notices that his pants fit him well, especially in the front.

Diane looks up from the computer screen and asks Miles "Can you come around and show we which file it is?" He does.

"Please pull up a chair and sit next to me, I know nothing about these things."

May thinks this is a good time to exit stage right. "Could I use your powder room?"

"Of course, dear, just go down the hall, second door to your right."

It's a beautiful room; she looks in the mirror and pictures Brandon. She feels flushed, splashes cold water on her face and sits on the edge of the vanity. She has the strongest urge to light up a cigarette, which is crazy because it's been four years since her last one. She spots a chair with a small end table holding an assortment of magazines and moves to a more comfortable position. Ten minutes go by and May thinks she shouldn't stall any longer, it would be too awkward.

When she returns to the office, she finds Miles sitting close to Diane. They have moved from the desk to a couch and are sitting side by side. He is examining a tray of men's wrist watches. "Diane has invited me to the Detroit Public Safety Foundation Annual Charity Auction as her escort, where she'll be donating these." There are seven pieces, Miles picks up a Breitling Navitimer and examines it. "Your husband wore all of these?"

"Not really, he was more of a collector. I would give him one on every anniversary or birthday. There was a lot more in his collection, but they were stolen during the robbery when he was murdered. Now, they only bring back tragic memories of the event and I want to get rid of them."

A call comes in on their radios and Miles stands up to leave. "Thank you so much for the coffee and invitation to the auction."

"I'm the one that should be thanking you. This video will ease my mind and I look forward to seeing you again."

In the car, May smiles and says, "Well, that turned out better than expected."

Chapter 14

May finds herself back with Dr. Salsburg, her official sessions as a police officer are finished but she has chosen to continue her visits. May feels comfortable talking with her and they have become close friends.

"Congratulations again on your Letter of Commendation. You seemed very tense when you were up there. Do you suffer from stage fright?"

"I know I appeared anxious but I think it was because I didn't feel like I deserved it. Now, I feel that I was reckless."

"The DPD believes you deserve it. They don't give out Letters of Commendation easily. You risked your career by going into a private residence like that. You must have been confident that the boy was there."

"I was, but I had nothing to base that confidence on, despite the fact that I told Miles I heard him call, even though I knew he was nonverbal. Even so, something told me that he was behind that door. Yet I was conflicted. I was putting not only my career on the line, but his as well. So, what was it that drove me to take the risk?"

"You have mentioned several times that you trust your instincts. How is it that you put so much faith in yours?"

"Apparently, it has run through my family tree for generations. My grandmother taught me to trust it. She says that it flourishes only on the female side. My mother prefers to trust the holy grail of science and doesn't believe in it. Whatever 'it' is, insight, clairvoyance, or sixth sense, it has always been near me, even as a child, like your favourite teddy bear. It gives a comforting feeling... my protector."

Chapter 15

Wayne State University is a sprawling institution covering over two hundred acres. Dr. Salsburg checks her phone to help guide her through the maze of buildings. The dotted trail leads her to the Liberal Arts and Sciences building. It is a prominent structure on the campus featuring a modern architectural design with a combination of brick and glass elements, giving it a sleek and contemporary appearance. Dr. Samual Levesque is the department head and has an office on the third floor of the five-story building.

The door to room 315 was open and she walks in to find two desks, only one of which is occupied by a twenty something year old man.

"You must be Dr. Salsburg, am I correct? Dr. Levesque is very excited to meet you. Can I take your coat?

Dr. Salsburg offers her coat and waits while it is hung up. She is surprised that the head of such a large department is sequestered into such a shared and small space.

She looks at the empty desk and asks, "Is Dr. Levesque delayed?"

"Oh no, that desk belongs to Janet Thompson but she's teaching a class right now. I'm Robert Armstrong. We're both postgraduates and honoured to be working for Dr. Levesque. He's waiting for you in his office right through that door."

Robert approaches the door and knocks softly.

"Come in." The door opens and Malinda sees Dr. Levesque who appears small standing behind his massive desk.

He quickly comes around with his hand outstretched. "So very glad to meet you Dr. Salsburg. Can we offer you coffee or tea?" He shakes her hand with surprising vigor.

"Thank you. It's quite cold out there and the wind is nasty. Coffee would be wonderful, and please call me Malinda."

"Certainly, let's leave the titles at the door. Robert, would you be so kind and bring us coffee?" Samual guides her to a pair of comfortable seats around a coffee table. "I've been looking forward to having this meeting since you called me last week, but what makes the DPD interested in folklore and mythologies? Does it have anything to do with an open case?" His voice raises an octave. "That would be so exciting!"

"I'm afraid I may disappoint you. I do a lot of my work with the DPD but this inquiry does not involve them." She sees the disappointment on his face and tries to think of a way to keep him engaged.

Her concern was not warranted as his expression quickly changed to one of acceptance. "Well, promise me that the next time an opportunity does arrive you will call me to assist you.

So, on to the reason for your visit. There has been quite a substantial study written on the subject you are interested in. He points to a row of books on the shelf to his right. I have authored these two books which will be relevant. I had Robert highlight several sections; they are yours to keep. As you probably know, folklore has frequently had its roots based in historical events and because they have been passed down by word of mouth, documented proof can seldom be found to corroborate them. In your particular case, the tribes located in West Africa, and especially in the area of Kingdom of Dahomey also known as Benin, have been fairly well researched. There is one legend that has remarkable connections to the one you described over the phone. It has its roots traced back to a relative of King Tegbesu, a local chief who ruled from 1728 to 1751. He had an adviser named Barunde, she was also his witch doctor and Sargeant at Arms. She was believed to have mystical powers. It is thought that King Tegbesu's daughter was sexually assaulted. In the King's anger he vowed that no member of his family would ever be left vulnerable again. He ordered Barunde to heal his daughter and forever protect the family lineage. This has never been proven, but there have been several documented cases where his family line has encountered mysterious situations only to be saved by miraculous events."

Their conversation extended well past what showed on Dr. Samual Levesque's calendar.

Chapter 16

There isn't an officer in the DPD that doesn't dread their annual evaluation. May includes herself in that group. Captain Masters is sitting at his desk and is looking over her file.

"You have had a good year. Your training officer says your performance was 'above expectations'. Of course, he might be slightly biased in that you saved his life. When we did this last year, you mentioned that one of your goals was to become a detective. Is that still the case?"

"Thank you, sir, and yes, that is what I want to be."

"Ok, I have put your name forward and Commander Williams, to my surprise, has approved it. You'll be able to take the detective exams. I must say that I've never had a trainee with only two years experience be given this opportunity before. It seems that you have someone cheering for you." He pulls out a large folder from his desk drawer and hands it to her. He tells her it is the Michigan Commission on Law Enforcement Standards (MCOLES) Reading and Writing exam. The duration of this test can vary, but it typically takes about 2 to 3 hours to complete. If she passes, she'll be slotted in for the next opening that comes up in the detective bureau. He continues "the tests are not easy, most fail the first time, so don't be discouraged if you don't make it. If you're preparing for the test, make sure to review the key areas it covers, such as vocabulary, spelling, punctuation, grammar, and clarity. You have two weeks to prepare before the next opening, so I suggest you take advantage and hit the books."

May is delighted with the news. It came as a total surprise. She ponders Captain Masters words 'someone must be cheering for you' and wonders if it was a random thought on his part or was there a deeper meaning. She thinks about who could wield that kind of power. Could someone be influencing the administration? Diane Stuart's name comes to mind. Did Miles ask her for her help?

"Thank you so much for this opportunity, Captain."

"You're welcome, you earned it."

Chapter 17

Every police officer applying for a position as a detective in the Detroit Police Department is required to take both oral and written tests. This is done at the Detroit Public Safety Headquarters located at 1301 3rd Street.

May arrives thirty minutes early and is told that she can wait in the reception room for Doctor Steelmen, Director of Human Resources. The interior of the building is ultra modern, each area separated by glass walls, some of the blinds providing privacy are open, some closed. May is offered coffee by her secretary. There is a small conference room visible across the hall. She sees that Deputy Commissioner Darius Brown – (3 star) Head of Detective Bureau, Commander Ji-An – (2 star) Detective Bureau Major Crimes and Captain Paul Jackson – Detective Bureau Homicide Division, are in a meeting. D.C. Brown looks her way. He says something to the others, and they look at her as well. She feels like she's in a fishbowl and has a crazy feeling that they have been talking about her.

Ten minutes pass, and to her relief Doctor Steelmen arrives. She is very pleasant and guides her into her office. She explains the process to May and gives her some background information about being a detective, long hours, disruptive family life, paperwork that never ends and may seem like a waste of time.

"Doesn't that sound like fun? Are you still interested?"

It's a rhetorical question and May just smiles. Dr. Steelmen tells her that the duration of this test can vary, but it typically takes 2 to 3 hours to complete. Dr. Steelmen escorts her to a small classroom down the hall. Two other officers are already seated at their desks which are separated by a wide margin. A small stack of papers and a pencil are on the desks. She takes her seat and looks around the room. She spots several cameras mounted on the ceiling. One of the other candidates looks her way but no words are passed. May takes her time and looks over each page before answering any of the questions. She found this technique worked well for her in college when there were no time restraints. She believes that psychological tests typically look for a specific answer but do so in a round about manner which is frequently revealed at the end of the questionnaire. The test was challenging but she had prepared and felt that she had done well.

Two days later Captain Masters calls her into his office and advises her that she has passed the test with flying colors, and a second meeting has been scheduled with Dr. Steelmen for her to complete the second group of tests, this being the oral phase.

May meets Dr. Steelmen in her office. Diplomas cover the wall and it's clear she's an academic. May asks if this is the normal procedure in taking the MCOLES. She had been told that it could take a month or longer to complete all phases.

"All the procedures are being followed, but some parts are being expedited. The mayor and council are under extreme pressure to bring down major crimes, so funds have been reallocated to hire more detectives. Let me explain how this next phase works. I'll be asking you five types of questions.

"Scenario-based questions: You might be presented with hypothetical situations that you could encounter on the job. For example, how you would handle a domestic dispute, a traffic stop, or a crime scene.

"Knowledge-based questions: These questions test your understanding of law enforcement principles, procedures, and laws. You might be asked about specific laws, departmental policies, or investigative techniques.

"Ethical questions: These questions assess your integrity and ethical decision-making. For example, you might be asked how you would handle a situation where you witnessed a fellow officer engaging in misconduct.

"Behavioral questions: These questions aim to understand your past behavior and experiences. For instance, you might be asked to describe a time when you had to make a quick decision under pressure or how you handled a conflict with a colleague.

"Personal questions: These questions help the interviewers get to know you better. They might ask about your motivations for becoming a detective, your career goals, and your strengths and weaknesses.

"Do you have any questions before we start?"

May tries to look confident "Looking forward to it, I'm ready."

Two hours later May doesn't feel so confident. None of the questions appeared to have an obvious answer. Every question seemed ambiguous or were designed to throw you off balance.

As she leaves the office, she meets one of the candidates that had taken the written test with her. She wondered if he had any idea what he was in for.

Chapter 18

"The Salad House again, you know a man can't live on that stuff. I'll be hungry again in two hours. Look, The Burger Bar is just around the corner, they have salads there."

May was driving, so house rules say she gets to choose. She argues a little more on behalf of The Salad House, but had always intended to go to The Burger Bar. She just needed a little more leverage.

"Ok, but you got to tell me every juicy detail about your gala extravaganza with Diane, deal? I mean every detail, what was she wearing? How was her hair, up, down? What was served? How was her speech? Did you dance? Every detail. And, if you miss one thing, and I will find out, you will end up eating rabbit food for a week straight, not that that would hurt you."

Miles says, "I told you already, we had steak. It was very nice."

"Ok, Salad House here we come!"

"319."

Miles picks up the mike, "319."

"Officer Sheppard is to report to head quarters and see Dr. Steelmen at the conclusion of your shift."

"319 Roger. What do you think? It's got to be about your test results."

May says "I don't know...but I'll tell you, it's going to be hard to keep my mind on the job."

May waits in the same reception room as her first two visits. A moment later Dr. Steelmen enters from her office with her hands extended. May expects a handshake but is surprised when she gives her a hug.

"Come in, come in" she leads her into the office and takes a seat behind her desk. "Please sit. I wanted to give you the news myself. It is policy to normally notify a candidate by mail on their test results, and we will send you a formal letter, but I wanted to ask you a follow-up question, is that all right?"

May's posture straightens as if she had just received a mild shock. *What kind of question would it be? Is this still part of the test?*

"Certainly"

"Well, I randomly create these tests based partly on the candidate's profile, each test is custom made, so I know that no one will have all the answers, you did though. You had a perfect score! How is that possible?"

"I'm very pleased that I did well. Most of the answers came easily but there were some I struggled with, like the behavioral questions. I had the answers, but how I came up with them... I would have to say, it came by instinct. I'm sorry, I just don't have a better answer for you."

"Well, congratulations, I really enjoyed working with you. Let's keep this confidential until you receive the letter which should arrive by end of week."

Chapter 19

May reads the letter for the umpteenth time. It's official, Detective has been typed in front of her name. She has been told to report at eight the next morning. *I need to get my ass in gear, but first, Sunday breakfast.* She prepares a soft-boiled egg on toast and a fruit smoothy. Ten o'clock and she is frozen in front of her closet. She has spent the last two hours, pulling out dresses, blouses, and skirts, that ended up being thrown on the bed. The closet is down to a pair of overalls that are covered with paint. *What does a newbie detective wear on her first day?* She expects to be scrutinized by her colleagues like she is in a row of camels at a South Arabian bazaar, especially because it was almost unheard of for a trainee police officer to be promoted to detective.

She picks up the phone and in resignation punches in Diane's number, she now has her on speed dial. They have become the best of friends and meet regularly to take in a show or have lunch.

"Hi Diane, it's me, I desperately need your help. I have gone through my closet and can't find a thing to wear for my first day as a detective and I start tomorrow."

"I got you covered girlfriend, I know a place, let me call the owner. I'm confident she'll open for us, and she has a tailor on call. I'm sure we'll find something appropriate for you there. I saw some very nice business suits when I was there last week. Bring your shiniest credit card, we are going to do some damage."

May was told to report to The Detroit Public Safety Head Quarters where she would be assigned. The building, originally the IRS Data Center and subsequently the MGM Grand Casino, also held the Fire Department, Forensics Department for the State of Michigan and the Detroit Medical Services.

She had chosen a dark navy suit from Armani; it was the picture a sophistication and speaks to both power and elegance. The blazer is expertly fitted, with a slightly cinched waist to accentuate the silhouette. It has a single-button closure, peak lapels, and subtle padded shoulders to convey authority. Made from luxurious wool-silk blend, it drapes beautifully. The tailor had even factored in the bulge for her service pistol. The matching trousers are slim-fit and cropped at the ankle for a modern touch. It is lined for comfort and made from the same high-quality fabric as the blazer. She added a silk blouse in a complementary light blue color. It has a tie-neck for a feminine touch. A statement handbag, from Hermès Birkin in a neutral brown color. She keeps her traditional jewelry of the elephant tusk necklace and her great-grandmother's ring but adds pearl earrings to complete the look. Low pointed-toe pumps added both comfort and confidence. The ensemble is polished off with a designer belt and a yellow silk scarf for a touch of color and flair.

Diane had told her it's not just about fashion—it's about feeling empowered and confident, and May knew that was what she was going to need. Every piece had been co-ordinated to impress. The tailoring was done overnight and delivered at seven the next morning. Diane had insisted on paying for the whole thing.

Monday morning May is introduced to Commander Ji-An, head of the Major Crimes Division. Her gallery wall shows she is highly educated, with degrees in Bachelor of Science in Criminal Justice from Wayne State University and a masters in accounting at Michigan-Dearborn. Pictures of herself holding awards, shows her moving through the ranks standing beside several former and present chief of police, and even one with the current governor, are all displayed in the same chromed frames.

Heavy-set, long black hair and wire rimmed glasses, Commander Ji-An looked like she had never left the office and never would. Her sanctuary was 21st century, chrome and glass, no documents were evident, she could not even see a filing cabinet. It all had to be on the computer, which was nowhere to be seen. May assumed it was under her desk. Only a large monitor and keyboard with a mouse was visible. She didn't even have a name plate like everyone else in the precinct. If it wasn't for her name on the door May wouldn't know how to find Commander Ji-An. May was not surprised when she walked into the office. She had done her due diligence when she had been given this opportunity to be interviewed for a detective position.

"Please sit-down May, I just want to give you a heads up." Commander Ji-An jumps right in, all business. "There is a vast difference between a street officer and a detective. It appears to be inevitable that once they take off the uniform and put on street clothes, they are hit with a sense of superiority, even arrogance. I'm telling you this because other than a professional hire from outside the DPD, you have been the only trainee to be parachuted into Major Crimes. This will be something new for your colleagues. There are those in the ranks that will require a period of time to accept the new reality, and they will, because they are professionals. I know that you have earned this opportunity. You have demonstrated excellent skills and dedication. Welcome to the unit and keep your head up."

Captain Paul Jackson begins the morning briefing by introducing May to the Major Crimes Division. May is escorted onto the stage by Commander Ji-An who presents her with the detective badge. Commander Ji-An approaches the lectern and tells her that it is more than just a symbol of authority—it's a badge of honor, commitment, and dedication to upholding the law and serving the community. The badge features a shield design with intricate detailing. At its center, is the official seal of the Detroit Police Department, showcasing the city's emblem and foundational year. Surrounding the seal, there's an inscription with the words 'Detective' and 'Detroit Police Department'. The badge's metallic sheen has a silver finish which adds to its dignified and prestigious look. It's mounted in a leather billfold.

For the novice detective, this badge marks the start of an important and impactful journey in their law enforcement career.

Chapter 20

At the conclusion of the meeting, Captain Jackson shows May around the division and introduces her to his squad. There are four other women detectives in the squad, surprisingly, all are white as are most of the detectives.

"You've been assigned to the Missing Persons squad." He walks her to a pod of four cubicles. "Your partner is Detective Judy Styles." They round the corner of a divider, and she sees her new partner for the first time. She hadn't noticed her in the briefing room twenty minutes earlier. Judy gets up from her desk and extends her hand.

May is hit with a wave of dread; certainly, this will put a spotlight on them both. Detective Judy Styles is white, barely five feet tall, blond curly hair. There is also a thirty-year age gap between them. They are night and day. Names flash through her mind; Mutt and Jeff, Beanstalk and Button, Sprout and Bean Stock or perhaps it will be the Odd Couple.

She is shown to her desk which sits opposite Judy's but is separated by a five-foot divider; on it she finds a voodoo doll made of black straw, it holds a spear in one hand and a shield in the other.

Judy says, "Looks like our resident prankster is already at it, try to ignore him." She smiles, but it's obvious to all that she is not happy. May is proud of her heritage and doesn't like having it mocked. Judy hasn't indicated who the 'resident prankster' was but what type of detective would she be if she wasn't able to find him or her. She picked up the statute which is quite heavy and started to walk around the floor. Major Crimes has over forty detectives and covers a lot of floor space. She passed several cubicles before the name plate of Fernandez pinned to a cubical catches her eye. He is sitting in his chair looking at his computer screen. *This is the guy,* she knows it. Fernandez knows she is there. He can see her reflection on the screen but does not turn. She senses his body tighten and it's a dead marker of his guilt. Without a word, she drops the doll in his garbage can which sounds like a gun going off, causing several detectives to jump out of their chairs and look over their dividers. Fernandez doesn't move and May waits a moment before walking away.

Several hours later, detective Fernandez is publicly summoned into Commander Ji-An's office. He is well known to be the squad jokester. Captain Jackson is also in her office.

"Detective Jesus Fernandez" begins the Commander, "You are the lucky candidate to be chosen to take the new diversity training class, and being the first, you will get to write a report on its benefits and how it will help you as a detective. You will then do a presentation to the rest of your squad. Thank you, Captain Jackson will fill you in on the details."

Chapter 21

Miles had arranged to meet her at the Trogen Inn. One of their regular dining spots. She spots him sitting at his usual booth facing the door with a coffee cup half filled. He looks out the window overlooking the parking lot so he could see her coming. Three empty packets of sugar have been neatly folded in front of him. "Typical of a detective, showing up ten minutes late, just like when a crime is being committed." He stands up and gives her a hug. They sit opposite each other. "Where is your new partner, Officer Williams, right?'

"He's at the dentist so no doubt I'll have to watch him drool and listen to him whine about his sore mouth for the rest of the day. You would think that having a tooth pulled was major surgery. One good thing though, he likes real food, not like a young recruit I once knew that only ate twigs and leaves. Now that you're a big shot detective is there a chance you will be picking up the tab for this lunch?"

May plays with the menu and only glances at it, she knew it from memory. "Not a chance, what does Diane think about your expanding waistline? We were at spinning class, and she mentioned it."

"Very funny, the woman thinks I have the body of a Greek God."

"Seriously, how have you been? How's the hip?"

"I've been going to physiotherapy for two months and it has slightly improved. The doctors say it won't get any better and I have been thinking about taking retirement. The injury makes me eligible for disability payments on top of the pension."

"Now there's a surprise, what will you do? I can't see you sitting on the porch in a rocking chair with a cat on your lap."

"I hate cats. Diane has some contacts at a private detective agency and I'm thinking of going there. Then I'll be a detective as well, but paid better than you."

"Sounds right up your alley, hiding behind bushes, being a peeping tom trying to catch the lonely housewife in a compromising position."

"It's sure good to see you again detective Mawusi Jane Sheppard."

Chapter 22

"Good morning, May, the coast is clear." May has always called Dr. Salsburg before entering the building. She has an inherent fear that a member of the DPD will see her making a visit on a psychologist.

"It's been two weeks since your last visit, you made some major changes in your career, how are you handling the change?"

"So exciting, so much to learn, a new partner, boss, procedures, dress. At times, a bit daunting, but surprisingly, what I like most is that we, my new partner Judy Styles & I, both like the same music. God, I'm so glad that I don't need to monitor the police scanner anymore, it was so depressing. I didn't realize how numbing it was. A home invasion, a four-car accident, burning homes, people trapped and worst of all officers down calls. The human element was gone; I was just responding to call signs."

"It sounds like you made the right choice. I'd like to talk a bit more about your reliance on what you called 'premonition' can we do that?"

"Yeah, I've been thinking about it more and more lately," May admitted, her gaze thoughtful. "I remember the stories my grandmother used to tell me when I was little. She had a strong intuition. She always said it helped guide and protect her through some difficult times in Africa." May made air quotes and smiled as she continued, "She believes in omens, signs, or what she calls 'forewarnings' to help her make decisions. I'm not sure if I buy into all of that, but I do believe in trusting my gut—it's never steered me wrong. And yet, I am not always comfortable with it. It seems that when it happens, I am not in control. At times it frightens me, these premonitions. If I understood why I have them I would be less afraid when it happens. I know this is not normal."

"Well, everything you have told me in all these sessions has showed nothing out of the ordinary. Perhaps it's time to try another approach."

Chapter 23

May hits the accelerator a bit harder in order to squeeze through the orange light. She's running late and the one thing she doesn't want is to keep her mother waiting. At her invitation, they had agreed to meet at Sashimi Bistro, a sushi bar near the university. Her mother had told her she would only have forty-five minutes between classes. As she pulled up, she could see her through the large plate glass window shaking her head in disapproval, fortunately it wasn't at her, she had her head down fully engrossed in something on her tablet. Probably an assignment from one of her students that had not met her expectations.

They greeted each other with a peck on the cheek.

"You're looking good, the new fashion is a big change for you. It must be quite a blow to the budget. Did you consider that when you moved from patrol to detective? The look is so different from what you normally wear. I mean, you have always had good taste, but this is more...elegant."

"Thanks, why are you still wearing your lab coat?" She doesn't wait for an answer. "I had some help from a new friend, Diane Stuart. Do you know her? She's on the board of a lot of charities and foundations." Her mother shows no sign of recognition. If it's not related to academia, it wouldn't be in her solar system. "Well, she travels in another direction from me as well. She recommended some boutique downtown so we went there and came out with this and two other outfits. She has great taste, but yes, it came as a shock and I certainly won't be able to sustain it. Back to Walmart and Target I'm afraid. How are things at the university, did you get that grant you applied for? Have you heard from dad lately?"

"The board moves slower than a glacier. I expect I won't get an answer this term, but all indications are positive. Your father will be home for dinner tonight, why don't you come over? I have a new post graduate student working for me, I could invite him as well."

"No doubt you have vetted him properly, comes from the right gene pool, good set of teeth? I'll pass but say hi to dad for me, tell him I miss him."

"I will, he wants a grandchild."

"When is his birthday again, I'll see what I can find."

"Please don't be sarcastic about your father's dream. He's supported you in every way possible. Having a grandchild who will carry on his name is his final wish. I was not able to give him more children, he..., we, thought we had the perfect child and placed all our hopes in you. He even told me that it would be ok if you didn't get married, and raised a child as a single mother. Can you believe that? It almost killed him to say it."

"I'm sorry, I want children too, I just need to get my career established and there's still plenty of time, I'm only twenty-five."

The waiter arrives with water, both know what to order, it's always the same, Tamaki and tea.

As they wait for their order to come, May eases into the reason for the lunch but she's not sure how her mother will react to her request. Her hands begin playing with the ring, spinning around absently.

"Isn't that your grandmothers ring?"

"It is, I like it. I have done some research on the inscriptions but have come up with nothing of interest. It's strange though, sometimes it starts to feel warm. Do you think there could be an element in its composition that I may be allergic to, or even a radioactive element causing it?"

"I doubt it, your grandmother never mentioned it and she wore it most of her life. If that's what you think, stop wearing it."

"But I like it, it ties me to her and my heritage."

"Well, if it's that important to you, I can see if someone in the Material Sciences can test it for me. I know an associate professor there."

"They won't damage it will they?"

"No, they'll just use the Atomic Absorption Spectroscopy or do X-ray Diffraction or who knows what other toys they have nowadays. None of it will affect it in anyway."

"Oh, thanks mom, you're the greatest."

Chapter 24

Despite the physical differences between Detective Judy Styles and herself, May likes her. Judy is eager to show May how to navigate the procedures and ultimately the politics of working in the Major Crimes Division which is vast. Major Crimes is divided into thirteen units, Special Victims, Sex Crimes, Domestic Violence, Child Abuse, Homicide, Fatal Squad, Public Order Crimes, Cyber Crimes, Auto Theft, HQSU, Arson, General Assignment Unit (GAU) and Missing Persons and they all report indirectly to Commander Ji-An.

May is driving listening to the sound of Simon and Garfunkel's, *Bridge Over Troubled Waters*, drifting from the speakers. Riding shotgun, Styles is on the phone. It sounds like she's talking to a doctor, but with the radio on she can't make out the conversation. From day one May has done most of the driving. She doesn't think that this is unusual, usually the rookie drives, depending on the preference of the senior detective. Something tells May, this is not the case with Styles and she has a sneaky suspicion that Styles has a problem seeing, especially at night. The glasses on her nose are the thickest May has ever seen.

Styles completes the call. "Let's visit the boyfriend again, ask him if he will voluntarily let us look at his phone. I want to swing by CVS, there is one on Market Street and pick up something."

Her phone rings again, "Yes, tomorrow at 3:15. We can make that appointment, thanks."

"Everything ok?"

Styles response is abrupt "Everything's fine."

Chapter 25

May sits in Captain Jackson's office listening intently as he summarizes her three month performance as a new detective in the Missing Persons Unit.

"If there's an area that you could improve on, it's your reporting. You need to focus on reporting in a more timely manner.

"You and your partner have raised some eyebrows with the command. Fourteen cases closed, three of which had gone cold. Your statistics are well above the other three teams in the Missing Persons Unit, not that everything is about numbers, but that's what the higher echelon sees. I see that you work well with others and I have noticed something else since your arrival. You're willing to test new approaches to your investigations by stepping out of your silo. In the past, units within Major Crimes worked their own cases in isolation. Sometimes to the detriment of the DPD. You've also engaged street officers in your cases. In the past that hasn't shown results, yet it seems to be successful with you.

"Congratulations, keep up the good work." May feels good about herself and leaves his office with a smile on her face.

Styles hangs up the phone, her expression is one of resignation. Her personality has changed over the last two months, she's been moody. Lately, she'll leave to do her own investigation, which is frowned on by their supervisor. They are to work as a team. It's Styles' responsibility to mentor the junior detective.

"How did your performance review go?"

"He appears to be happy with it, made some comment about timeliness on reporting."

"I have never seen Jackson happy, that's something new. As for reports, he wouldn't be happy if we solved a case using a crystal ball and reported it before it even happened."

May smiles "Let's go check the morgue. I got a text message that they received six new bodies over the weekend, three of which don't have identification. One of them fits the description of Marty Alexander."

"You go ahead, there's something I have to do on my own, but I'll walk you to the elevator."

As they pass a small conference room May spots Mat Strouse pointing to a rolling digital white board. There are three other detectives with him. The room is crowded, several tables covered with empty coffee cups, stacks of paper, printers and computers.

"What's going on in there?" asks May.

Judy stopped and looks at where May is pointing. "That's the General Assignment Unit or GAU. They are working on three cases with similarities. The correlations became evident when a new algorithm was installed into the Michigan State Criminal Database. A second search showed there could be more cases. All young white girls who were abducted, some kept for a day, some for two, but all received small tattoos, then released. It's believed that it was perpetrated by the same person."

"When did this happen, I haven't heard anything like this on the news?"

"That's been the problem, the incidents happened over the last year with months between them. The girls were gone for such a short time that it never hit our radar, but things have changed since the last victim. The tattoos have become larger and cover a larger area of her body. The girl was kept for three days. The perp warned her that if she showed his 'art' to anyone, if he sees it in the news, or on Facebook, anywhere, he will find her and skin her alive. It was to be seen by his eyes only. The girl was so traumatized that she wouldn't allow pictures of the tattoo to be taken. The picture they have of her is from her driver's license."

May watches as Mat writes something on the board, he is the same detective that was heading the triple murder five months ago.

Chapter 26

The unmarked cruiser pulls up to the curb at the entrance to William Milliken State Park. Detective Styles pulls out her badge and shows it to the patrol officer who is waiting for her on the curb. She reads his name, Romans, from the name plate on his uniform, another small favour owed.

"He hasn't been a problem, we kept the crowd away."

They walk a short distance to find an old man standing on a park bench. He is wearing two shirts and no pants.

She addresses Officer Romans, "you didn't find his pants, did you?"

"No Ma'am, I was walking the park when an older lady reported it. He offered me a plastic card with his identification on it, and it had a note on the back with your name and number. I haven't called it in. Don't see a need, he hasn't made a fuss and the lady wasn't upset. Just being a concerned citizen."

"We're out of time. Time is the enemy. Before it's too late you must...." He stops in mid-sentence when he spots Detective Styles standing in front of him.

"Hi dad, out for a stroll? Let me help you down, it's time to go home."

"Yes, yes, time, time to go!"

She helps him off the bench "What did you do with your pants dad? Did you leave them somewhere, or did you forget to put them on?"

"I have on my shirt."

"Yes, but you also need to put on pants. You look much better in your suit."

"Thanks officer, I won't forget it."

She places him in the back seat of the cruiser and drives to a nearby thrift store. A short time later she comes out holding a pair of blue pants. "Put these on dad, they should fit." A block further they arrive at Matheson House. "You're home dad. Have you had lunch? Why don't you go to the dining room, and I'll have lunch with you? I'm just going to the office to have a chat with Mrs. Phillips. I will be back soon."

Chapter 27

May is apprehensive and a bit excited. Dr. Salsburg has arranged for a hypnotherapist to attend her next session. She was to meet him today. She had been told that hypnotherapy involves several key steps to guide an individual into a state of deep relaxation and heightened suggestibility. It starts with an initial consultation. The hypnotherapist gathers information about the client's issues, goals, and medical history to tailor the session to their needs. This is followed by Induction. This step involves techniques to induce hypnosis, such as Eye-Fixation, fixating the gaze on an object until the eyelids become heavy. Progressive Relaxation, focusing on breathing and relaxing the body from the feet up. Imagery, visualizing a safe and comfortable scene. Deepening, the hypnotherapist deepens the hypnotic state using techniques like progressive relaxation, visual imagery, and deep breathing. Posthypnotic Suggestions, while in a deep hypnotic state, the hypnotherapist makes suggestions to address the client's issues, such as behavioral changes or symptom relief. Awakening, the hypnotherapist gradually brings the client out of the hypnotic state, ensuring they feel alert and refreshed.

Mr. Timmons is waiting in Salsburg's office. It appears that he has been there for some time, two empty cups stand on the coffee table. No doubt May has been the subject of their conversation. He is older than she expected yet, he springs to his feet to greet her. He has thick grey hair and a quaint mustache that covers most of his upper lip. He is very short and more than thirty pounds overweight, most of it hanging over his belt. Salsburg makes the introductions. Mr. Timmons greets her warmly. Within minutes she finds him to be very likable, obviously a critical characteristic required for his profession.

He prefers to be called by his first name, John. He goes over the procedure and it's remarkably similar to what Salsburg has already explained to her. May thinks they must have read the same book. He stresses that hypnotherapy is a collaborative process, and the client remains in control throughout the session.

John suggests that she lay down on the couch and make herself comfortable.

He begins to tell her a story, his voice is soft.

"May, can you imagine yourself at the beach? It's a warm spring day. You can smell the ocean air and hear the surf." His voice is so soft. It reminds her of a feather falling onto a pillow like she saw in a commercial. It has a slow rhythmic tone, like the sound of waves lapping gently onto the sandy beach. The story is about birds. They are colorful, flying over the water in a gentle breeze. They don't even need to flap their wings, just glide. The up current from the ocean is sufficient to keep them airborne. He tells her that it's ok if she wants to close her eyes and envision them. The story goes on for about five minutes.

"Why don't you take a little rest and watch the waves come in for me."

It turns out that she is very receptive to his suggestions, and it takes little time before he begins to ask her questions.

"May, tell me how you are feeling."

"I'm feeling relaxed John, comfortable, everything is good."

"Excellent, Dr. Salsburg is going to ask you some questions now. I'm going to move to the next room to give you and Dr. Salsburg some privacy, but I will be close by, is that ok?"

"That's fine."

Mr. Timmons leaves the room and Dr. Salsburg takes over.

"Good morning, May, do you remember our last few sessions? We talked about your premonitions and how you felt uncomfortable about having them at times?"

"Yes, I...trust them, maybe too much, so when I have them, it's scary. Like walking on ice, you know you can walk on it, but will it always hold you? I have always had premonitions, but now, as a police officer, the consequences of trusting them become more serious because I could be putting other lives at risk."

"Can we go back to a few of the times you felt like you were putting others at risk, perhaps when you and officer Styles interrupted the gun deal?"

"I guess. I was ... "*Leave her alone, this is none of your business!*"

Salsburg is taken aback, she immediately straightens in her chair. The voice came from May, she is certain, but it was not hers. It was female, and very firm, demanding. It had a heavy accent, perhaps from someone that came from Africa.

She sits quietly, considering what she just heard and the implications. Could this be a gag? Does May have her cellphone on? It is her policy that they be turned off at the beginning of each session so that they won't be disturbed. There is a sign on the wall reminding her patients to do so. She looks at the door where John exited with suspicion. It was not his voice. Besides, he was a professional, and if this was a ruse it would end his career. She got off her chair and approaches the door. It has a peep hole through which she can see if there is anyone in the reception room. John is flipping through a *Motor Trend* magazine. She returns to her chair and sits next to May.

"May, are you ok?"

"*She is fine, just leave her alone, you don't know what you are doing!*"

Salsburg takes another minute. She questions if she should end the session and call in John to get her out of hypnoses. She looks at May, she appears to be laying comfortable, her breathing is slow and study.

She decides that there is no risk at present and continues.

"Who are you?"

"You may call me Adwoa Boateng."

"I am Dr. Malinda Salsburg, I am a psychologist treating May Sheppard."

She notices that May is twirling a ring around her finger in an absent minded manner. She had not noticed the ring before, it must be something new.

"Her real name is Mawusi, it means 'in the hands of God' and I know who you are and what you are trying to do. You are meddling in something that is beyond you. Why are you interfering, I'm looking after her."

"She came to me for help."

She picks up her cell phone and checks the time. John had advised her to keep the first session to a minimum.

"Thinking about recording this on your phone?"

Salsburg looks at May, her eyes have been closed the entire time, how did she know that she had picked up her phone?

"I don't think she would like that, you know how paranoid she is about these sessions getting back to the precinct."

There had been a split second where she had thought exactly that.

If this wasn't a hoax being perpetrated on her, then she could come to only one other conclusion, Disassociated Identity Disorder or DID. It was previously called Multiple Personality Disorder. The proper name for what is commonly referred to as 'dual personality disorder'. DID is characterized by the presence of two or more distinct personality states or identities within a single individual.

The thought of treating someone with DID excites her, but Adwoa might be right. She will need to do more research before diving further in.

"Adwoa Boateng, would it be ok if we talked again in the future?"

"I haven't talked to anyone in a long, long time other than my hosts. It may be something different to explore. Let me think on it, but for now, I have had enough."

"Adwoa...are you there?" She is greeted with silence, only May's soft breathing can be heard. "May, can you hear me?"

"Yes doctor."

"I'm going to ask John to come back into the room and bring you back, is that all right with you?"

"Sure, that's fine."

Salsburg goes to the door and asks John to come in. He sits next to May and begins to take her from her sleep.

May sits up unaware of what has transpired over the last half hour. John leaves the room after determining that May is fully awake and clear headed.

May asks Salsburg "How did it go, do I have any secrets left?"

"It was a very interesting session, I think I would like to discuss it with you at our next meeting, is that ok with you?"

"Sure, see you next week?"

Chapter 28

Styles and May have been working on a missing person case for the past three days. May starts showing annoyance because Styles keeps pulling her disappearing act and doesn't tell her where she's going. May suspects that it's personal business. As a new detective, protocol requires her to be with a partner when following up on the case outside the office. She plays with her ring in frustration and closes her eyes. A small spasm causes her to tip over her coffee cup, spilling a few drops of coffee onto the profile of the missing girl. She selects the file on the computer and sends it to the printer located just outside the conference room now confiscated by the GAU.

She looks through the glass and sees pictures pinned to a display board of the three young girls. The printer beside her makes a small beep indicating the job is complete. She removes the paper and looks at the picture seeing that there are similarities to the three pictures on the display board. They are all white, approximately eighteen to twenty years of age. So is May's missing person. Under each picture there is a column of information about each of the victims, date of birth, date they were abducted and date released. The abductions started just over one year ago. From the time they were taken to the time they were released was gradually extended. All the girls where involved in the arts in some fashion. Matilda (Matty) Freeman, her missing girl, was also a student taking classes in liberal arts at the University of Michigan.

May sees Detective Strouse on the phone pacing the conference room. She knocks on the glass to get his attention. He turns and waves her in.

Strouse recognizes her from the time she was at the triple homicide and delivered the critical witness that helped close the case.

"Detective Sheppard, what can I do for you?"

"Please, call me May. I have a missing girl that is remarkably similar to your three victims." She hands him the summary page which has Matilda's picture on it.

"You're assigned to Missing Persons now, right? Why do you think she was abducted?"

"Her roommates, they are the ones that reported her missing, say that she had no reason to run off. She was doing exceptionally well on a full scholarship, had no serious boyfriend, and there didn't appear to be anything out of the ordinary. We have checked for her everywhere, home, friends, etc. Her parents are abroad and planning to come home."

"Ok, send me your report. I'll have someone from the team look at it."

She's not sure if she has been dismissed. She goes to the board and looks carefully at each of the victims.

Strouse notices her interest. "From the little information we have been able to obtain, mostly from the medical staff, it appears there is some commonality in the tattoos."

May has a strong feeling come over her. *These women are now connected in more ways than their common interest in the arts. You know it is true, tell him they are being used to tell a story.*

She whispers to herself, *"I have nothing to base that on, I haven't even seen any of the tattoos."*

Strouse turns to her and askes, "What did you say?"

"Oh. Sorry, I was just thinking out loud. "I mean, they all look so similar, if the tattoos are getting bigger and they are by the same person, maybe they are incomplete, part of a bigger picture, like a story."

Strouse gives her a curious look. "Thank you May, good work. If you find any more, let me know."

She leaves, she likes working in Missing Persons, but this, this would be exciting!

Chapter 29

Deputy Commissioner Darius Brown – Head of Detective Bureau, Commander Ji-An – (2 star) Detective Bureau Major Crimes and Captain Paul Jackson – Detective Bureau, Major Crimes are in a meeting to review the GAU case. Their Public Relations department has advised them that rumors are circulating within the media about a serial tattooist and that it will soon become a feeding frenzy among the press.

They had invited Detective Strouse, who is heading the investigation unit, in for an update. Strouse tells them that they have been checking alibies from every tattoo artist in the city but there are over thirty shops, and each shop can have four or more employees. As well, there are countless former inmates that have learned the profession while in custody. The main stumbling block has been the lack of co-operation from the victims. The perpetrator has always had them blindfolded and kept them sedated to the point their description of him is of no value. He has also been effective in creating enough fear that they will not allow us to take photographic evidence of the tattoos. So far, the victims have not been seriously injured during their captivity, but each victim's tattoo has covered more and more of their body. He appears to add to each tattoo like he is trying to tell a story. Strouse gives them the bad news that a fourth victim has come forward. This one had been kept for four days and was currently recovering at home.

Darius shows his disappointment at the progress. Strouse senses the mood in the room and is desperate to give them something positive in his report.

"There is one promising lead that we are following up on. Another girl that fits the victim profile has gone missing for 4 days now."

Ji-An asks, "Was this highlighted in the MSCD report?"

"No it wasn't, because it fell outside the parameters. The new detective, May Sheppard, in Missing Persons brought it to our attention."

Ji-An looks up May's file on her tablet and makes a quick notation next to her personnel file. She slides the computer tablet to Brown who is sitting to her right. May's father's name and his occupation have been highlighted '*Homeland Security – Head of Office for State and Local Law Enforcement*'. Brown gives a knowing look to Ji-An. Jackson notices the exchange but is kept out of the loop.

The Detroit Police Department has been trying to improve relations with Homeland Security since it was established in 2003.

Strouse continues to tell the small group about the possible new victim. Her residence wasn't listed as being in Detroit, and therefore did not show up in the MSCD data base search. He explains the progression of attacks and the pattern clearly shows that there will be more. With the discovery of another victim, he will need to cover even more ground. He asks for more resources. Brown immediately sees the benefit of having someone high-up within Homeland Security, especially within the department of State and Local Law Enforcement, connected to the case. This, if managed right, could be a boon to the department.

The State and Local Law Enforcement division is responsible to administer training to all law enforcement as well as approve funding for special equipment and programs. They do not have direct control over the state law enforcement but do control the amount of funding each state will receive. The golden rule still applies, those with the gold, makes the rules. Three years ago, the DPD had requested additional funding to train a second Special Weapons and Tactical Unit (SWAT), but the request had fallen on deaf ears. There had been several other requests for funding, but none seemed to make it past the gate keepers at Homeland. May's father would be the person to approve or reject the requests.

Deputy Commissioner Darius Brown was sitting at the head of the conference table and casually poses a question to Captain Paul Jackson.

"Captain, with the discovery of this new victim by Detective Sheppard, do you have any objection to adding her to the GAU team? I think we can back fill her position while she is reassigned."

The answer to the rhetorical question momentarily runs around in Jackson's mind. Why would someone in Deputy Commissioner Brown's position offer additional resources? Jackson would normally need to fill out and submit stacks of requests for additional manpower that would take a week to filter up through the chain of command before it was approved or more often, rejected. He quickly analyzed the situation and could come up with only one answer. This time, wrongly so, that the GAU was currently made up of all male detectives. With another victim reported there was going to be a lot of scrutiny as to why there weren't any female detectives involved in the case, especially with all the victims being female.

"Absolutely not, adding a female detective to the team would definitely be the right thing to do, wouldn't you say Detective Strouse?

Strouse stumbles for the right words, he too is surprised at the offer of additional resources coming from the Deputy Commissioner. He likes May but is concerned about her level of experience as a detective. Nevertheless, he needs the extra manpower and knows better than to refuse it, especially when it's offered by Darius Brown. He'll find a use for her, even if it is just to catch up to the endless paperwork.

"Absolutely sir, the current team has had difficulty with interviewing the victims, they have given us almost nothing. They might be more receptive to questions if they are asked by a female detective."

Chapter 30

He looked at the canvas, stroking it ever so gently with his surgical gloves. Once again, he wished he could take them off, but he knew that wouldn't be possible until the work was completed. This time, there won't be any mistakes.

There had been defects with the previous products that he hadn't anticipated. They had looked perfect, but once the wrapping was removed and upon closer examination, he discovered imperfections and blemishes. The first two attempts had been a disaster. The sad part was that it had accomplished very little but he did have an opportunity to practice. Almost all of his work had been done on males thus far. He found that the female skin reacted slightly different to the needle, so, that was of some value. The third one already had a tattoo on her buttocks, which hadn't been visible until he removed her bikini. It was a butterfly. He had considered removing it with a laser, but that would have been too time-consuming. He had invested a considerable amount of time and expense in obtaining the canvas, so it could at least be used to test his design in the more challenging areas. If nothing else, he would gain experience. He tried to incorporate the tattoo into the design, but after fifteen hours, the results were disappointing.

He sourced a fourth piece, which was flawed as well. Upon removing the bra, he discovered scarring. It was obvious that breast enhancement had been performed. The fifth also had a scar in the same area, this one most likely from a biopsy for breast cancer. That had come as a surprise for someone of her age. Nevertheless, it was an opportunity to test out the front of the image. From now on he would search their medical history before going through the trouble of abducting them.

The latest one, his sixth canvas, was perfect in every way, at least that is what he could see. He had done extensive work over the four days. Then it began to vomit, could the anesthetic be the cause? It happened again the next morning. The realization struck him hard, he quickly went to the drug store and purchased a test kit. It was positive, she was pregnant. His work would become twisted beyond recognition. He had to be true to his art or else, what was the purpose? His people, the inspiration for his masterpiece, spoke of their culture and one of its basic beliefs was that the unborn was sacred. He would need to stop. The extended use of anesthesia could cause it harm or even death. Unlike the others, he would drop it off near a medical facility. Then he would continue his search for new material.

Chapter 31

Dr. Fredrick Washington had suggested that they meet in the small conference room at the Athenium Suites Hotel. He had booked a room there because it was convenient for him as he was a guest speaker for the American Psychological Association (APA) Annual Convention which was taking place within walking distance of the hotel. Dr. Salsburg was also attending the conference.

"This is fortuitus, I much prefer to consult in person, don't you?"

"Your presentation today was well attended, thank you so much for taking the time to talk with me" replies Salsburg.

"You're welcome. Your case is intriguing. I have had several cases involving DID as I mentioned in my presentation, but only two where the alter manifests itself, ancient or venerable, and acts as the primary's guardian unbeknownst to the primary."

Ninety minutes later Dr. Salsburg left the room satisfied that she could continue to engage with the personality calling itself Adwoa Boateng.

Chapter 32

May stands up and looks over the divider between her and Judy's workstation, it sits idol, again. She has not been told where she went or when she'll be back, but she has a good idea. She looks again at the picture of Matilda Freeman. Young, white, beautiful. She could grace the cover of any magazine. She flips the page in the file and checks the notation she has made. Two names have been highlighted in yellow marker. Phillip Depree and Brad Walland.

According to her roommates these two young men independently and actively have been trying to date Matilda, without success, since the start of the semester. She doesn't have an address for either of them but has tracked down their schedule. Phillip has a lab scheduled in one hour at the Physics Building and Brad has a class in theology scheduled just after lunch. If she leaves now, she can catch them both.

She takes her cellphone out of her purse, hoping that Judy will pick up. They could meet up at the University. She is about to hit speed dial when her desk phone rings.

"This is Thema Eastman, I am Commander Ji-An's assistant. Would you be available to meet her in her office in ten minutes?"

For a moment she wonders if Thema has dialed the right number. "Certainly, can you tell me what this would be about?"

"She'll explain it to you, thank you. Please be prompt."

May grabs her purse and goes to the washroom. Immediately she becomes circumspect. Was it because she approached Strouse without going through her partner? It made no sense. As she makes her way through the maze of cubicles, she feels the eyes of her co-workers following her. They all seem to know what this is about, adding to her apprehension. She can't come up with any reason to meet with Ji-An. She wonders if she should drop by Captain Jackson's office first, just so that he is not blindsided by this meeting. She walks past his office and finds it empty. She scans the floor and sees no sign of him.

May is wondering what this is about. 'I haven't done anything wrong...I hope, shit, I'm so new to this, I could have made a dozen mistakes and not even know. But I just had a great performance review.'

She finds herself standing in front of Thema Eastman just in time to come out of her daze.

"Hello detective, go right in."

Ji-An is reading a report and looks up. "Good morning, Detective, please have a seat. Thank you for making the time on such short notice, I know you have a heavy caseload."

Her desk is acrylic with only a computer and an open three inch binder on it. She closes it slowly, places both hands on the desk framing the binder as if she is about to offer it up. A long title is printed on the cover in bold letters '*Grant Application for Land Mobile Radio (LMR) System to Homeland Security Services*'.

She lets out a small sigh, and with resignation says, "This thing.... I've been working on for almost a year. Our officers need to have the best communications systems available, but you know that, coming from the streets, how critical our dispatch system is. It was submitted to HLS six months ago and still not a word in response. I just can't seem to find a way around the gate keepers!" She pushes the binder to one side in a dismissive manner.

She continues, "Sorry about bending your ear on that, not your concern. How are you doing in Missing Persons?"

May gives all the right answers, excited, happy to add value to the unit, likes her co-workers.

Ji-An gives a grunt. Not the response she had expected.

"The GAU has asked for additional resources. The media is about to get their teeth into this tattooist case, and you know what that will mean, more scrutiny. I understand that you have identified a possible victim in the abduction cases that the GAU is working on. Captain Jackson thinks you might be able to fill that need."

May's face brightens; this was totally unexpected. To be involved in a major case was what being a detective was all about, at least it was for her.

Ji-An takes out the metaphorical wet towel and slaps May across the face.

"I, however, just don't think that someone so new to a high-profile case is wise for you or the department. If something goes wrong, even if it doesn't, the fact that we haven't announced that we have a serial tattooist roaming the city abducting young girls will bring a hailstorm of anger down on the DPD and put our relationship with the public in the proverbial toilet."

Ji-An pauses, then continues "May, do you think you are ready for this opportunity to help not only solve this case but also to help the DPD in other matters? If your answer is yes, report to Detective Strouse on Monday morning."

Ji-An doesn't state what she means by *other matters*.

Ji-An repositions the binder back to its original position and randomly opens it. She lifts her head and looks at May as if to say, 'are you still here?"

May looks at the binder, stands up and leaves the room without either saying another word.

Chapter 33

May leaves the office with a mix of emotions. At the top is the feeling of being used by Ji-An to get access to Homeland, the other is excited to be brought into such a big case.

"Hey Mom, I'm just leaving now. I should be at the house in about thirty minutes. Did you need anything for me to pickup at the paint store other than the drop cloths?"

She had offered to paint the spare bedroom before her cousin came over from Honolulu for a two-week visit. It would be a good time to discuss the proposal by Ji-An before Monday.

"Great, we'll have breakfast before we start. Your father has conveniently had to stay over in Washington so I'll need your muscle to move the dresser. How he figured out that I had planned to do this is beyond me, but he always finds a way to get out of helping to paint."

Her mother has baked cinnamon rolls and has sliced and buttered them before placing them in a frying pan. The aroma is unmistakable as she walks into the kitchen.

It doesn't take long before her mother broaches the subject, she sees her daughter is struggling with something. May tells her about the offer by Ji-An and asks her what her father would think or do.

"You know how much your father loves you and if you ask, he will move heaven and earth for you. He is so proud of you. You have told me yourself how badly the emergency services needs a new dispatch system. Lives depend on a reliable and clear way to communicate. It sounds to me that Ji-An is being ignored by the big wheels of government. Don't be upset with DPD, this is the real world. Everyone needs a little help from time to time and this could be a win-win situation."

May's eyes well up. She knows that not only does her father love her, her mother does as well, but has trouble expressing her emotions. May gets off her chair and gives her mother a hug.

Her mother's response is to pull the ring from her purse and tell her that the tests have come back with interesting results. Test results show the ring is composed primarily of four elements. While three elements, namely gold, platinum, and osmium can form alloys with each other under specific conditions, incorporating a fourth element, xenon, into such a mixture would be extremely difficult due to its lack of reactivity. This would have been virtually impossible in the seventeenth century. In practical terms, creating a stable compound that includes all four elements, even today, is not feasible with current technology.

Her mother looks at the ring for a moment. She doesn't believe the stories of the shaman like her mother and grandmother, but this ring, this...it's something tangible. I am a physicist. The science of it, that, I can relate to. This ring should not exist.

Chapter 34

Monday morning May finds herself in the conference room occupied by the General Assignment Unit. She has arrived early in the hope that she will be able to review the data collected on the case before the rest of the detectives arrive. She is not surprised to find Strouse already completing the necessary paperwork identifying her as the new member of the team.

"Good morning May and congratulations. You can have this desk," as he points to an old metal desk stuck in the corner next to the coffee station.

She wonders if this will be her role!

She's surprised when he tells her the victims refuse to have pictures taken of their tattoos. Partly because they are ashamed and partly because the perp has warned them that if he ever sees or hears that his work is on public display, he will find them and skin them alive.

"Somehow, he's been able to instill so much fear that they won't show their tattoos, not even the ones on their arm. We have interviewed the doctor and nurses that are currently treating Teresa Malborne, the second victim", he motions to the picture posted on the board, beside her name there is the number two.

"It's from her driver's licence. The medical staff has seen the tattoos but are reluctant to even describe them because the patient has insisted that they tell no one, so, we have the patient confidentiality to deal with. The doctor has said that Teresa has been traumatized to the point of being suicidal. Apparently, the few times that she remembers being conscious he had repeatedly told her that his art is only for him and her to see. We do know that it covers most of her back."

After a moment he begins again. "It's basically the same story for all three victims. Brenda McDonald, she was the first reported victim, is very religious, so we tried having her priest convince her to talk to us, but without success. She is sequestered in her home and won't talk with us anymore. We have been told by her parents that once her body has healed enough, she is planning to move to a convent.

Strouse moves to the coffee pot and refills his mug, which has a U.S. Marines logo on it. "Since you identified Matilda Freeman as a possible third victim, we have expanded our search in the data base going back three years. There may be two more incidents that could be related. Both girls were from the street, addicts, and not involved in the arts world. Their tattoos were small and were of flowers and standard symbols. They were both released the same day. We have tried to locate them, but they seem to have vanished.

May finally asks, "What do we know about our suspect?"

"Considering we have been at this for three weeks, almost nothing. No description, we don't even know his race. We do know, if the other two possible victims are part of this case, he has been at it for almost two years. No idea as to his motivation, if any. The victims are all white, young females, considered to be very beautiful. Abducted by a male, drugged and strapped to a hospital gurney. Once they wake up, they described it like a hospital room, white, monitor equipment, IV stand. Large moveable lights like the ones in surgical rooms. They all had intravenous lines in their arms, but they couldn't tell what was in the bag. They were not able to identify their location, no distinctive sounds of trains, boats or cars. They were drugged the entire time and awake for only short periods. Teresa thought she saw a camera mounted on a wall. All the girls remember waking up covered head to toe in a disposable biohazard suit that you can buy at any hardware store for under forty dollars. Locations where they woke up vary, in the woods, alley, one was in the park laying on a bench. They do remember his voice, no accent, strong, and of course his description of what he would do to them if they showed his art to anyone. How he induced so much fear into these young girls..." his voice trails off, without answering his own question.

Strouse hands her a binder, "Here is everything we know so far. Take whatever time you need to familiarize yourself with the case and report back to me for your assignment when you're done. Welcome aboard."

Chapter 35

Mat sits at the local watering hole with his former partner, Shelley. His second beer, that he believes will be his last, sits half empty. Her Pinot Grigio has droplets of moisture on the wine glass, untouched.

Mat says, "I like May and she's proven that she has good skills. I can see that there's a need for a female detective on this case. It could be our last chance to get co-operation from our victims, but a twenty-five-year-old with only two years experience and virtually none as a detective, boggles the mind. When it comes to doing the interviews, she won't even accept having another detective with her. She had the gall to already insist on that. Can you believe that! She is already telling me how to do a proper interrogation."

Shelley picks up her glass and takes a sip. "The nerve of her, but she could be right. If you're going to take a different approach to 'interrogating' a victim, you may want to let her run with it."

He gives her a look, "I didn't mean that! He takes another sip from his beer. I don't think she's up to it." He pauses a moment "I think what's bugging me the most is that the paper pushers have dictated who will be on my team. When I asked for more resources, it was you I wanted. I mean, that has never happened. Why would they saddle me with her?"

"Wasn't it her that brought you the latest victim?"

"*Possibly* the latest victim, right now she is a missing person, but yes, she is likely another victim of this psycho."

"Yeah, that's interesting. The buzz on the floor is speculating about that. But you have her now, and you might as well make the most of it. If she's their new golden girl, better to help her up than push her down."

Chapter 36

May takes *The Book* to a small meeting room and spends most of the day reviewing it. It is well organized. Investigating a case involving multiple abductions where victims are tattooed, held for days, and then released, repeating again within a month is highly complex. Such cases require coordination across multiple law enforcement agencies, forensic experts, behavioral analysts, and possibly federal authorities, depending on the jurisdiction.

The first few pages are a summary of the case. It looks like Strouse updates it daily as the case progresses. May believes this is mostly for the administration and Public Relations Department should they ask for the current status of the investigation. Each section has its own tab and subsections. Along with the section title, there is a description and sometimes an example of what was expected.

The next tab is titled 'Initial Response & Victim Recovery' which details the first contact with the victims: Each identified victim is treated as both a survivor and a key witness. Officers document their condition, emotional state, and immediate statements. A medical examination is conducted to check for injuries, infections, or drugging. Photos are taken of tattoos, restraint marks, or any signs of mistreatment. This last section is empty with only a notation that the victims refuse to be photographed.

Next is Victim Interviews & Profiling: May is surprised when she reads the content of this section. It is structured by the order in which the victims where identified. It covers 'Structured Forensic Interviews'. These were to be performed by a detective trained to avoid re-traumatization. Three of the detectives within the unit were listed. May wonders what type of training was involved in re-traumatization and makes a note to investigate. She also lists the names of each one of the detectives hoping they will expand on the notes in *The Book*. There are notes on each victim with the questions and their answers. Victims are asked about their abduction experience, sensory details (sounds, smells, surroundings), and any identifying factors.

Timelines are reconstructed: When and where were they taken, tattooed, held, and released? Had they noticed anything suspicious before the abduction, anyone following them? The questions seemed endless. May wondered what questions had not been asked and she couldn't think of any.

Tattoo Analysis: Is the tattoo a brand, a symbol, or an identifier? Does the tattoo match known gangs, cults, or trafficking symbols?

Handwriting/style comparison—was the same person tattooing all victims? Tattoo ink composition and method (was it done professionally or crudely?) This section too was only a note stating that the victims refused to show the tattoos. They had been asked if a police artist or a friend that she trusted could do a sketch, perhaps she could at least describe them. Each one refused. No amount of persuasion could change their mind.

Common Patterns in Victim Selection: This section was well documented. Each victim's history going back several years filled *The Book*. Were the victims from similar backgrounds, locations, or demographics? Any links between them (social media, workplaces, hobbies)?   Did they receive similar instructions from their captor(s)?

This section had extensive notes; it showed that the victims had been awake just prior to being released. They had all been forced to listen to what they believe was a recorded message describing what he would do to them if they showed his work to anyone. The recording was played over and over again. Along with the recording there was a horrific video of young girls being tortured and skinned alive.

Behavioral & Criminal Profiling: Understanding the Suspect's Pattern; The fact that victims are held for days and released suggests control rather than impulsivity. The tattooing could indicate ownership, ritualistic behavior, or a psychological mark of dominance. Are they being "marked" for a purpose (e.g., gang initiation, trafficking, experiment)?

Possible Motivations: Power & Control: The abductor enjoys exerting control over victims. Ritualistic Behavior: Could be part of a belief system, cult, or personal obsession.

Psychological Conditioning: Could be testing how victims react over time.

Group vs. Lone Actor: Is this one individual or an organized effort? So far, there is no evidence that there was more than one perp. No one heard or saw more than one perp during their abduction or release.

Geographic Profiling: Where were the abductions, holding locations, and release points? Mapping the pattern of these locations helps narrow down suspect areas. Instructions were given on how to create the map. Each abduction had been pinned to the city map. It covered a radius of 4 miles. Red dots showed the abduction points, and green dots showed the areas where they were found.

May wondered if the instructions were for the purpose of creating a data base for AI analysis in future cases.

Evidence Collection & Forensic Investigations, Forensic Tattoo Analysis Ink: composition tested to find common sources (e.g., a specific brand used by certain artists). If crude or homemade, it may indicate someone with prison tattooing skills.

One victim had a small skin scrape performed while in the emergency ward. The doctor had suspected a possible infection and thought it might have been caused by the ink. Test results indicated the ink was homemade, as there were no matches found in the database. Homemade ink indicated that the perp may have served time and possibly learned his art in a penitentiary. There was a computer list of the ink composition used at establishments and penitentiaries that performed tattooing services. There were no matches found.

The following tab is titled Medical Evidence: It has subsections for DNA swabs, fingerprints, bodily fluids, and fibers collected.

DNA & Trace Evidence: Victims may carry fibers, hair, or skin cells from the abduction site. Were they clothed the same way when released? Any unusual materials? DNA testing was negative; it appears that the victims were scrubbed before being dressed in the hazmat suits.

Medical Examinations & Toxicology: Were victims drugged during captivity? This section provided significant data; residual drugs show that Dexmedetomidine (Precedex) was used on all victims tested. An investigation was ongoing to locate the source of where the drug was made and distributed, as well a list of purchasers was being developed. The list includes all pharmacies, hospitals, and emergency clinics. They were listed in alphabetical order and covered twenty pages in *The Book*. There had been no sign of sexual abuse.

Were there signs of malnutrition or dehydration? Other than the damage done to the skin, (which was serious) all of the victims appeared to be in good health.

Surveillance & Traffic Data: Surveillance is checked to track individuals entering and leaving the location of the abductions and the release points. Any cameras near abduction or release points? It appears that our perpetrator has scrutinized the area before the abduction because no cameras are located. License plate readers (LPRs) may identify vehicles used. 'No' was checked in the provided box.

Social media analysis: Did victims interact with someone online before being taken? None found, but there was commonality in their search history. All victims showed an interest in art. A list of URL and social media sites was listed along with dates and times. Between the victims, the list exceeded four hundred and ninety entries over the last six months. An analysis of the pattern showed that most were related to the classes the victims had been taking.

Suspect Identification & Investigation: Comparing with Previous Cases; Have similar abductions occurred locally or in other regions?

Two cases were reported: One in 2001, Pharr Texas, Suspect apprehended and in custody at Walls Unit, Huntsville TX. Second case was in 2015, Mobile Alabama, suspect was killed by police.

Checking law enforcement databases for offenders with past abduction or branding behaviors. Ongoing, three abduction cases on file, all perpetrators in custody or deceased.

Tattoo Artists & Underground Networks: Investigators interview tattoo artists about customers who requested unusual tattoos.

Checking illicit marketplaces where forced tattooing or branding may be associated with trafficking. Ongoing, none found to date.

Undercover Operations: If a pattern suggests a specific area, officers may go undercover to interact with potential suspects. No undercover officers currently assigned; however, the following higher educational institutions have their own police force. They have been advised to be on the lookout for individuals showing undue interest in white females currently involved in creative arts programs. Wayne State University, University of Detroit Mercy, College for Creative Studies (CCS), Wyne County Community College District, Marygrove College. The names of the supervising officers and their phone numbers were listed along with the date and time they were called for updates. Strouse had had one of his detectives follow up each day in the hopes of keeping the abductions high on the minds of the officers.

Media Strategy & Public Assistance: If needed, law enforcement may release limited details about the tattoos to solicit tips from the public.

Search Warrants & Suspect Interrogation: Based on collected evidence, search warrants are issued for suspects' homes, businesses, and digital devices.

Interrogations are conducted with behavioral analysts present to detect deception.

Charging the Perpetrator(s): Charges may include kidnapping, assault, branding, unlawful imprisonment, and other related crimes.

Ongoing Monitoring & Preventative Measures: Law enforcement keeps an eye on similar crimes.

Community awareness campaigns help prevent future incidents.

Artificial Intelligence Analysis (AI): This section showed only; Analysis Inconclusive, insufficient data provided.

The list of items continued with witness lists, friends and boyfriends list, suspect lists, some of them reached more than thirty pages. There were graphs, timelines, expense sheets, it went on and on. Some fields were complete, many were left blank.

May closed *The Book*, picked up her notes and went to see Detective Strouse. He had sure kept his squad busy.

Chapter 37

Strouse sits across from May, his egg sandwich half eaten. "Tell me your thoughts based on what you found in *The Book*."

"I thought your team has covered a lot of ground."

"I don't need an ass kissing rookie. I brought you in to get a fresh perspective!"

"Ok, I think the victim interviews where botched, and I'm not sure you'll be able to recover from it."

"You're right, on both counts, I did blow the interviews, and I won't be able to fix it. So, you will have to. According to the assistant prosecutor, without the victim's co-operation we have no chance of getting a conviction and he walks free. We need the victims to show us those tattoos, we need them to agree to testify, and we need photographic evidence. If we don't get it, then the best we could hope for would be that we find him, and he tries to fight it out with us. That too will be considered a failure in the eyes of the DPD brass. I don't like to fail. So, put together a plan on how you'll reinterview these girls and get back to me."

Chapter 38

May knows that she needs to take a different approach than that of her counterparts. She doesn't think her being a woman will be enough for them to open up.

"Hello May, this personal or professional? I don't have you scheduled until Thursday."

"Professional, you can bill the DPD."

Dr. Salsburg pulls up her calendar on the computer "I can fit you in at three, will that work?"

May hesitates and Dr. Salsburg suspects May wants to meet immediately. As usual, May has made her call a block from Dr. Salsburg's office.

"Ok, come on up."

Three minutes later May enters and is warmly greeted. "Congratulations, I heard you got moved to the Tattooist case."

"Yes, how did you know? Don't tell me, you have inside information that you can't reveal. That's what I need your advice on." May fills her in on the details of the case.

"Based on what you described, it could be associated with social anxiety or shame-related phobia, depending on the context. In some cases, this fear might stem from catastrophizing—an irrational belief that revealing the secret will lead to severe consequences—or from feelings of guilt or vulnerability. It sounds like it is deep seated and will take extensive therapy to understand its roots and find coping strategies."

"Unfortunately, I don't have the time for a traditional approach. "Can you give me the Coles Notes version on how I can get these girls to talk with me?"

"In that case I suggest using some of the same approach that is used in the treatment of PTSD, first do not apply pressure. Don't flash the badge, you are not an authority figure. Don't lie. They will certainly shut you out. Start with your concern for them, see how they are doing. Build empathy. This could take several visits. Find their comfort zone, locations they are familiar with. It doesn't need to be quiet; it could be a playground with the laughter of children or their own bedroom. Build rapport. You 're both women, share your story, try to focus on art, or other common interests, show her your tattoos, what they mean to you. They may feel ashamed of theirs; you can be proud of yours. You would love to see theirs. The tattoos are hers now, to do with as she pleases, not his. Tell them that you are meeting the other victims and stress that they are victims of a vial act. Try to work in the idea that they may want to meet each other, it could be comforting.

"Tell them, the perp is disgusting, a piece of filth, there is overwhelming full-time resources committed to finding him. Move the needle away from fear to anger. You already know a lot about him. His medical experience, he is a loner, he has made a lot of mistakes. He will be captured or killed. Which would she prefer? Take it in steps, first is his capture, and focus on what you need from them to accomplish that piece. Don't mention identifying him or asking them to pick him out of a lineup. Nothing about testifying in court. It could be too overwhelming for them.

"Normally you would leave the girl with the strongest support group till last. They will try to protect her. Getting the first one to co-operate will be very important to getting the rest to come forward. But considering the time restrictions you may want to reverse that. Just be prepared to sidestep these people, know who they are, do the research. Try talking with their girlfriends first. They may have already talked with the victim, they should be supportive to apprehending him for no other reason than self preservation, this guy is still out there, and they could be next."

Chapter 39

May takes Salsburg's recommendations to heart. Should she ask her to do the interviews? She has given solid advice and would be better than her to implement it. The problem with this approach is they would have different goals. Dr. Salsburg would focus on the victim's need. Hers is on capturing the perpetrator. No, she would have to do it herself.

She begins putting her plan on paper and will present it to Strouse.

The next morning, she sits with Strouse right after he has updated *The Book* and directed the team to their assigned tasks. She goes point by point, explaining the strategy for each step. She knows that he will have concerns about how long this will take, but to her surprise, he just nods his head.

"Ok, just remember we have been looking more into your missing person, Matilda Freeman, it's now very likely that she too has been abducted, odds are by the same guy. He has held her longer than any other victim so far and I'm concerned that we could be adding a murder charge to the list soon."

Chapter 40

Friday night and everyone is in good spirits. Diane and Malinda have invited almost all of May's old street squad and many of the detectives to a party to celebrate her promotion now that she has passed her probationary period. The girls chose The Twisted Sisters Bar and Grill because of its convenient location to the precinct. The place is packed with blues and suits and there are cheers and applause in appreciation of Judy's performance of The Eurythmics, *Sweet Dreams*.

Miles makes his way through the crowd with two margarita glasses, giving one to May and one to Diane. "She has the voice and the moves."

May spots Detective Strouse walking in, she had noticed his absence and wondered if he would make an appearance. Immediately a wave of guilt hits her, how could she be celebrating when Matilda Freeman was alone, lying strapped to a hospital gurney in a dark room somewhere?

The sound of whistles and howls brought her back. Miles was taking her glass and substituting a fist full of dollar bills into her hand. He pointed to the stage where a stripper was well into his act. Malinda was pushing her forward. She could only see him from the back and noticed that he was wearing tight blue jeans, a police cap, no shirt, no socks or shoes. He had his legs spread, poised with arms over his head. The biceps and deltoids cried out under the stress of the pose. The skin glistened with perspiration. Magically, the female officers moved to the front. He looked better than a Greek god. The music, "You Can Leave Your Hat On" by Joe Cocker seemed to grow louder to keep up with the approval of the crowd. He turned and slowly began to undo the buttons of his jeans. Somehow, he was able to slide them off. Obviously, he had extensive practice, revealing a jock strap that had been decorated with bright red lips. He jumped down from the stage and was swarmed by a crowd of officers waving money. The rush pushed May into the performer. They were eye to eye for the first time. May recognized the dancer as Brandon, Diane's security man and driver. Brandon in a bold move proceeded to immediately kiss her and she did not resist.

That night she was grateful for Brandon's offer to drive her home as she had had too much to drink and her head was spinning.

Chapter 41

May develops a plan. She will interview each victim based on their personality profile that the team had created. She feels fortunate because Detective Strouse didn't have the benefit of this information to work with before interviewing them. It was his interview that was the basis of the report. May meets with Mat again to review her approach to doing the interviews. She believes that if she does this right it will break open the case and she is filled with apprehension, she wants him to buy into her approach. He approves but does remind her that they will need hard evidence.

She calls up Brenda McDonald, the first reported victim, introduces herself and schedules a follow up meeting with her for the next morning. Next, she drives to the Wayne State University to meet up with Jill Waxman, a close friend of Brenda's. They talk for over an hour in the cafeteria. Unbeknownst to her she is being watched. Jill tells her how important Brenda's relationship with the catholic church is. It has helped her get through the ordeal enough for her to start returning to her studies and take up classes again. May asks the name of her church.

Father Stone knows Brenda well and is eager to assist in any way possible. He takes her for a tour of Sacred Heart which was built in 1875 and is on the National Register of Historic Places. He points out several pieces of art that have been restored by Brenda.

One more stop before she is ready for tomorrow's crucial meeting. She picks up her phone and hits speed dial.

"Good afternoon, what's your pleasure, personal or business."

"It's both. I need to borrow something that's very important to you, but I promise to have it back tomorrow in perfect condition."

Chapter 42

Dr. Salsburg had recommended that the victim with the strongest support group be interviewed last. Unfortunately, May's first and best opportunity at interviewing a victim had just that. Brenda lives in a residential area of Detroit with her mother and father. The house, and the property it sat on are pristine. Brenda is Mr. and Mrs. McDonald's only child. May is welcomed in by both parents. Signs of their faith are prominently displayed throughout the house.

"That is a beautiful cross you are wearing." says Mrs. McDonald.

"Thank you, I got it from a very close friend, it meant a lot to her as well."

After her introduction to Brenda, May suggests a walk to the local park. It's a beautiful day; the area is safe and quiet. Brenda readily agrees, anxious to leave.

On the street, Brenda says "They have become so protective it's suffocating. That's the primary reason I decided to resume my classes. Do you know that they actually checked you out before agreeing to the interview!"

May smiles "My father is in law enforcement; he wouldn't let me date until I was eighteen. Every one of my boyfriends were put through gruelling interrogations. It was so embarrassing."

Their walk takes them past Sacred Heart Church. May stops for a moment to admire it. "Its beautiful, can we go in?"

"Would you like to go in? I can show you around. This is my church and I have done some restoration work for Father Stone. I'm sure he wouldn't mind."

The tour lasts fifteen minutes and ends in the sacristy. "You have done some amazing work. Can we sit here and have our talk?"

Brenda looks around the room and smiles "Sure I like it here, what would you like to discuss? I can't think of anything I haven't already told Detective Strouse."

"You've been very brave and I would guess that your faith, along with the protection your family gives you, has helped. The other victims are not as fortunate as you. They don't have that going for them. Some are still in the hospital. One girl's parents are overseas and won't make it back until Thursday. The other girls need help to get through this. Our faith requires that we give it to them. Would you consider meeting with them and discussing your treatment at the hands of this monster? I have been told by a good friend who is also a psychologist that sharing traumatic experiences with someone that has gone through it themselves is helpful to both parties."

"I hadn't thought of it in those terms. I don't see any harm in it. Do you think it will really help them?"

"I'll see if they would be willing. One thing I don't understand though. The other victims have told us the size and location of their tattoos and they had been held prisoner longer. Why do you think he let you go when he did?"

Brenda is silent. Finally, she says, "He scares me so much. I still can't sleep without medication. The images of what he will do if

I show or even discuss the tattoo is burned into my mind, but he did not say that I couldn't talk about my own tattoo."

"You had a tattoo before the abduction took place?"

"Yes, my parents don't even know about it. I got it when I was sixteen. It's on my left cheek below the panty line. It was a blue butterfly, but you can't make it out now because he destroyed it, made it into something else that's unrecognizable. I guess it didn't work out the way he wanted it to, is all I can think of."

"Do you recall anything more about the actual attack?"

"Not really, I was driving home from the Detroit Institute of Arts. I knew I needed gas, and I had to take a break, so I stopped at a gas station. It was raining and I pulled up next to the bathroom on the side of the building. When I came out, I was hit by bear spray. I got it straight in the face and I couldn't see or breathe. It burned so bad. That's all I remember. I must have passed out. After that I found myself drifting in and out of consciousness and my ass really hurt. I somehow knew what he was doing because it felt the same as when I had my tattoo done earlier.

"When I first woke up, I thought I was in a hospital. All white, lots of medical equipment. He walked into the room, wearing scrubs, gloves, face mask and cap. I seem to see him a little clearer now. From the little bit of skin I saw, I don't think he was white, more like, Hispanic. He may have had a slight midwestern accent. That's all I can remember right now."

"Thank you so much for meeting with me. It must be horrific for you to bring those images back to life."

"I have been thinking on what you said, about meeting the other victims, and my duty to God. If you can arrange it, I'll do it."

Chapter 43

After dropping off the gold cross to Malinda, May meets with Terica Tramell, one of the forensic team members specializing in taking crime scene photographic evidence. May takes her for coffee and explains her dilemma, that the victims have the right to privacy, dignity and respect. So far, the courts have not permitted the police to force them to have photographic evidence taken or have warrants issued against them.

May asks, "Do you know with any level of certainty, that I can give them some assurance that their pictures won't be duplicated and end up on the internet?

"We use only digital cameras now. The best I can do is encrypt the image or add a password to the file folder. I can also trace who has had access to the images and add a watermark. But once the password is revealed, the photos could be duplicated, printed or photographed. There are a lot of people that will be granted access, not just the members of the GAU, but our bosses, assistant DA's, their staff and everyone in my department. It happens all the time, this place leaks worse than a sieve.

"The only thing I can suggest is that you move away from digital and go old school. Don't even use a regular camera with film because they can be photocopied or duplicated. There is some new technology I have recently heard of at the last Sutterfest Conference I attended in St. Louis and it was something that the

FBI was developing. Do you remember the old Polaroid or Instax Cameras? They developed the film inside the camera, so with these you don't have to worry about negatives floating around, but they can still be photocopied. Well, at the conference, they talked about something similar but once the image was developed inside the camera, it could only be viewed if you placed a transparent shield over the picture. That shield was unique to the film in the camera which held only twelve pictures. Even if you had the shield and the image, you would not be able to copy it, it would only come out white. That way you could give the girls the shield and the photo could be secured with the DPD. This gives the victims control over who sees them. It was developed as a high security tool. I don't have access to it. You would need to know someone high up at the FBI."

"That sounds like a great idea, thanks so much."

Chapter 44

She feels the vibration of her phone and pulls it out of her pocket. The display reads 'unknown caller'.

"Good morning, my name is Robert Henderson, is this May Sheppard?"

It's a pleasant male voice and sounds like he's in a good mood. "This is she. What can I do for you Mr. Henderson?"

"Oh, please call me Rob. I actually have something that you might be interested in. I work at the university and was privileged to have been shown your ring by Professor Nilton who did the metalogic analysis on it. I am an associate professor of semiotician, do you know what that is?"

"So, you're the new 'Robert Langdon'?"

"Don't I wish." She hears soft laughter. His voice moves up an octave and she can sense the excitement in his voice. "Well, I hope you don't mind, but I did some preliminary research on the inscriptions. They are very unique, dating back to the seventeenth century. I was wondering if you would be interested in a meeting to hear about my findings?"

"Perhaps, Rob, how did you get my number?"

"Through Todd, Professor Nilton, we're friends and he got it for me. He called your mother and told her about me, asking if you would be interested in what I had found and if it would be ok to contact you."

"I would be very interested in hearing what you discovered but I don't have my calendar with me. I'm on my way back to the precinct, can I call you back in a few minutes?"

"Absolutely, the precinct, are you in law enforcement?"

"Yes, I'm a detective."

"How exciting, I look forward to hearing from you. You can call me at this number, it's my cell."

"I'll get back to you soon, thank you Rob."

She had her calendar on her phone, but she wanted to chat with her mom first.

At the precinct she first updated *The Book* and checked in with Strouse, then did a Google search on Robert Henderson. Everything appeared to be kosher. He didn't look at all like Robert Langdon, the fictional character in Dan Brown's book *The Da Vinci Code.* Associate Professor Robert Henderson was pleasing to the eye. She found his picture on the fraternity website. He looked to be of mixed race, his skin color slightly darker than her own. Good strong facial features, clean shaven. That was a plus. A full head of hair but nicely trimmed. He looked to be about her age. Just one more thing to check.

"Hi mom, quick question, I just wondered if you know a Robert Henderson, he works at your university? No...ok, his name just came up in a conversation. Talk with you soon. Bye."

She waits an hour before calling him back.

"Hi Rob, it's May Sheppard, if you are available, I would love to hear what you found. Would this afternoon work for you? I need to go out of town tomorrow and don't know how that will affect my schedule thereafter."

"I have a class to teach this afternoon. Would you be receptive to meeting over dinner?"

She is liking the sound of this. "If you let me buy. You did all the work and it's the least I can do."

"Great, text me the location, how does seven sound to you?"

"Perfect, see you then."

Chapter 45

She opened her closet which had developed a malevolent appearance; dark, with an open mouth, threatening to growl at her. She hates flipping through its contents. It was exhausting. When she becomes filthy rich, she'll hire a personal shopper/dresser to handle this. Her clothes would be laid out for her every morning. In addition, her personal shopper would have access to her calendar so that if evening wear was required, she would take care of that as well. Business or personal, definitely personal, maybe a bit sexy? She ops for a yellow bare back dress, which compliments her brown skin. Low heels, his picture didn't indicate how tall he is so better to play it on the safe side. Her hair hung in cornrows eight inches past her shoulders. Just her usual jewelry.

She had made reservations at *Parc* in both their names. Diane Stuart had taken her there once before. It was situated in Campus Martius. *Parc* blended European culinary traditions with wood-fired grill flavors. It offers stunning views of the cityscape and a vibrant indoor-outdoor dining experience and its pace of service was in line with the relaxing atmosphere. You could enjoy a conversation without having the table next to you overhearing.

She arrived five minutes early and circled the parking lot. Typically, Wednesdays were not busy and there were plenty of empty parking spaces. There, a late model dark red Mazda matched the licence number May had researched. No doubt Captain Paul Jackson would point out that using the department resources for personal reasons is against DPD policy. Tell that to Commander Ji-An when she suggested that May use her personal connection to influence Homeland. So, bite me! Anyway, he was here, one more trip around the block and she could go in.

She was guided to a table for two by the hostess. Rob was dressed in a casual summer suit, dark blue with white stitching, a soft peach shirt. The tie was white and had a diamond pattern that appeared to be made of silk. He stood smartly, offering his hand and quickly drew back her chair.

A young waiter appeared, filled water glasses, offered them menus and asked if they would like to order a beverage. Rob looked at her, she gave him a blank stare, testing to see if he would take the lead.

"Canadian whisky and water on ice please."

She ordered a Long Island Iced Tea.

"A detective, that must be an exciting line of work."

"I'm quite new at it, I got promoted from a patrol officer only five months ago."

"Which is better, detective or patrol officer?"

"For me, detective by far, I found that a patrol officer's life was routine, driving the same area day after day, only changing when you needed to react to a situation. Detectives need to solve mysteries, using their brains.

"How about you, what is it like being a professor?"

"Associate professor. Its probably the same as your mother. Teaching young minds, hopefully about something they themselves are interested in. It too becomes routine after a few years. But then something comes out of the blue, like your ring, and in a sense, you get to be a detective as well. Perhaps I'll publish a paper on it. In the academia world you need to publish or you never make professor."

Their drinks came.

She raised her glass in a toast. "To the next *Angels & Demons*. I have never dined with a famous author before."

They touched glasses. He had a great smile.

"Tell me about your upcoming New York best seller."

He bends down and retrieves a notebook from a leather satchel opening it to the first few pages. It looks to May like the metalogical results of the ring. The next eleven pages show the ring from different angles. Each one fills the page. They are hand drawn in exquisite detail. He must have viewed the ring under a microscope.

"Did you draw these yourself? They are beautiful."

"I do a bit of sketching in my free time, mostly historic buildings."

He continued and his voice betrays his excitement. This must be something very important to him.

"Every one of these symbols, there are twelve of them, six on the inside and six on the outside, come from different areas within the continent of Africa. This alone makes it groundbreaking. No one has ever documented anything like it. Ancient symbols always come from a specific area, like a language."

He has drawn every one of the symbols onto its own page, giving a written description on the opposite side.

"I have identified nine of them, every one is unique. I hope to discover the meaning of the rest. The amazing thing is that they all tell a story."

She transfers her attention away from the book to her ring which she had been inadvertently twisting around her finger. She suddenly became chilled and gave a slight shudder.

He stopped his oration to look at her. "Are you ok? Here, take my jacket." He quickly stands, removes his suit jacket and drapes it over her shoulders.

"Thank you, please continue. This is so fascinating. My grandmother told me it had quite a history."

"A history that goes back a long way, back to the seventeen hundreds."

"You said that it told a story."

"Yes, but it's incomplete and I'll need to find the meaning of the other symbols to see if there is an ending. It appears that it was made in Western Africa in or about that time. The story revolves around a young girl, who had a connection to some influential people. She was attacked by a group of men from another tribe who raped and murdered her. Because the village people would not identify those responsible, all the men over the age of sixteen were taken and enslaved to work in the mines until their deaths. There were over sixty men between the ages of sixteen and sixty at that time in the village. None ever returned home. That girl must have been very special to generate such a strong reaction by the people in power at the time. The high priestess ordered the ring to be made as a reminder that no woman in the village should ever be left vulnerable to man."

"That's an amazing story. My grandmother studied the ring as well. She got it from her mother and gave it to me. You might want to talk to her and see if she can help with your research. She has an amazing collection of art and artifacts from that region. I'm positive she would love to hear what you have discovered."

"That would be fantastic, would you be available to make the introductions?"

She smiled in agreement.

Chapter 46

"Hi dad, how is Washington? Have you got a minute, there's a couple of things I want to talk with you about."

"Hi May, I sure do, what's on your mind?"

She goes into her story, focusing on the issue of the camera. "So, have you heard of anything resembling it, does it even exist?"

"Actually, it does and I had a presentation on the latest hardware technology around security three months ago."

"Do you think I would be able to borrow it for a day?"

"Let me check to see if it's available. It's a rare tool and you would need to be very careful with it, we wouldn't want it to fall into the wrong hands. What's the other thing you wanted to discuss?"

"I think it would be better to do that in person, so can you call me back about the camera ASAP?"

"I can do it right now, hold on while I make a call." May is on hold just long enough to complete her doodle. "Hi, you'll need to come to Washington to pick it up tomorrow. They won't send it out by courier for security reasons. Can you make it here for breakfast, then we can talk about that other thing?"

"Fantastic dad, and thank you, see you tomorrow."

Chapter 47

DMC Detroit Receiving Hospital is where Teresa Malborne is being treated. GAU identified her as the second victim. She was found wandering in Rouge Park dressed in a disposable environmental suit just like the one Brenda McDonald was wearing. She gets a brief update from Dr. Ula on Teresa's medical condition. She tells her that physically Teresa has healed, but her mental state has marginally improved. She will soon be transported to a mental facility where she'll receive further care. Dr. Ula provides guidance for the interview.

Teresa is enrolled at Wayne State working her way through a Masters of Fine Arts (MFA) degree with Photography as the primary. Dr. Ula has kindly taken the time to do the introductions. Teresa appears calm and Dr. Ula leaves to complete her rounds.

"Thanks again for meeting with me Teresa. I understand you'll be leaving here this afternoon. How do you feel about that?"

"I'm looking forward to it. The staff are wonderful, but the place still looks, smells, and sounds like a hospital. I can't get a good night's sleep. They tell me that Infinity Hope Center is very nice, not at all like a hospital."

"I understand that you are a shutter bug so I brought you the latest *Aperture* magazine."

"Oh, thank you, there isn't much to read relating to my master's degree here in the hospital. I'm starting to get behind in my studies."

"I heard you'll be able to attend classes online at Infinity Hope. Is that right?'

"Yes, and I'm really looking forward to it."

"I was talking to Brenda McDonald yesterday and she was quite helpful. You are familiar with her? She was wondering if you would be interested in getting together, perhaps at your new location, would you be interested in that?"

"If it's ok with Dr. Hamilton, he'll be my primary physician at Hope."

"Good, I'll clear it with Dr. Hamilton, let Brenda know and make the arrangements. Do you remember meeting Terica Tramell, she works at the DPD, the crime scene photographer?"

"Yes, she was nice, she wanted to take pictures of my tattoos, but I can't do that. He'll find out. He knows everything. He's always watching."

May can see that this line of conversation is starting to upset her so she quickly moves forward.

"Terica is really interested in photography as well and told me about a new type of camera that was being developed by the FBI. It's called 'Safeguard'. Have you heard of it?"

"Yeah, but it's just a myth. It's rumoured to be a security camera but no one has ever seen one, not even my professor. They say it's old school, analog technology that can't be copied. It sounds like something out of James Bond."

"I'm picking one up tomorrow, would you be interested in seeing it? I can bring Brenda, and the two of you can play with it. See if you still think it's a myth."

Teresa's eyes lit up like it's her first Christmas and she has just spotted a tree full of great presents. "That would be amazing, if it's true. You can do that? It would go a long way to completing my master's thesis."

"Good, I'll see you tomorrow after you get settled in."

Chapter 48

May exits the hospital on her way to her two-year-old emerald green mustang when her phone rings.

"Hi Judy, what's up?"

"Ready for some good news? I just got a call from Gerald, Matilda Freeman's older brother and he says she's been found and that she's all right. Apparently, she went out for a hike in Balduck Park, fell and broke her foot. It was three days before someone found her. Other than her foot, she's ok."

"That is good news. I'll update Strouse and let him know she's off the victim list. Why did it take three days to find her? That's a popular hiking area so you would think that someone would have spotted her earlier?"

"Yeah. I asked her brother the same thing and he said that she prefers the more challenging routes and got lost."

"Have you talked to her or seen her?"

"No, I just got the call and he said not to bother. He'll pop by the precinct tomorrow to fill out the paperwork. She just got out of surgery and has her foot in a cast."

"Ok, what hospital is she in?"

"DMC."

"Ok, great, see you soon. Bye"

May begins walking to her car and as she goes to open the door, it happened again, that feeling she can't describe makes her turn around. She knows that something is not quite right. She locks her car door, turns around and heads back to the hospital.

"Hi, can you tell me what room Matilda Freeman is in?"

"She's in ICU. It's on the sixth floor, turn right when you get off the elevator. You'll need to talk with someone at the nursing station to find out where she is."

May is the last to get into the crowded elevator which stops at four of the six floors giving her time to think about what the hell is going on. Were there complications with the surgery? Her brother said she was already out of surgery. May was no doctor, but thought putting Matilda into intensive care after setting a bone seemed to be unusual, especially for someone in their prime and in good physical condition.

Again, she asks, "Can you tell me where I can find Matilda Freeman?"

"Are you family?"

May pulls out her badge. "I see, she's in ward three, but she's not allowed any visitors on orders from her attorney."

"What can you tell me about her condition?"

The nurse, or doctor, May doesn't know for sure, she could be either one, begins typing on the keyboard.

"I'm afraid there is a block on the medical file as well detective. You would need to speak to an administrator to get access."

"This is a criminal investigation, why would there be a block on something as simple as a broken foot?"

"Well…, I've seen the patient, and I can tell you that it wasn't a broken foot."

"Can you tell me if her brother has been here?"

"She came in by ambulance and I haven't seen anyone. She was wearing white disposable coveralls and had her driver's license and wallet, which had emergency contact information inside. We were able to contact her brother and he was the one that put a block on her medical records. Apparently, he has power of attorney and is also her lawyer."

May called Judy, "Hey Judy, did Matilda's brother Gerald, give the number where he could be reached?"

"I can get it. The call came through the switch board so give me a second. Local 946-2421. Why, what's going on?"

"There's something wrong here. I was at DMC visiting one of the victims when you called. So, I thought I would drop in on Matilda while I was here. It appears her injuries are not in line with what he reported."

Judy says, "I'll give him a call back, see what's going on."

"Hold off on that will you. I want to update Mat on this before we contact the brother."

"Ok, you got the ball but keep me updated on this will you?"

"I sure will, thanks for the heads-up call."

May calls Mat and gives him the news.

"Good work, I'll have one of the team check out this Gerald Freeman, see if he's real. I'll do the phone trace. If it's a cell we can see if it's still active. Stay there for now and see if you can find out anything else. Talk to the administrators to see if you can lift the block. Tell the nurse not to tell anyone that the DPD is making inquiries."

Chapter 49

On the drive home frustration had boiled over. How was she supposed to get the evidence if she couldn't even get access? She grabbed the steering wheel so tightly that her hands started to cramp. That's when it came to her.

Yes, it was unsubstantiated, but it was a theory. In hindsight one she probably shouldn't have told Strouse about until she had at least seen one of the tattoos.

That afternoon the team sits in the conference room, each giving an update on what they have been doing.

Strouse had ordered a uniform to be stationed outside Matilda's room and was told to keep an eye out for anyone making inquiries about her. The cell phone was traced and ended in a dead end. It was a burner purchased at a 7 Eleven on 5145 Anthony Wayne Dr. in Detroit. A pin marked the location of the store on the map adding to the cluster of pins forming around the area of Wayne State University. A blowup of the area had been made to give more detail. The phone, a Samsung S23FE, had been purchased six months ago but only activated yesterday. It had gone dead right after the call to Detective Styles was made. The phone had been paid for in cash. Strouse points out that this shows extensive planning on the part of the suspect. The video, retrieved from the store security system was played for the team and shows that three cellphones were purchased that day. Only one person paid cash, a man approximately six feet tall and dressed in a hoodie. The area around the 7 Eleven was searched but no additional cameras were located with an image of the suspect.

May reports that she had found a nurse in emergency who had performed the trauma assessment before sending Matilda to ICU. The nurse confirmed that Matilda did have extensive tattoos on the front of her body and that they appeared to be new. To her, it looked like they were incomplete. She had looked at them for only a second and couldn't describe them, only that they were very complex.

"I also went to the lab where a technician told me that her blood work showed that she had the hormone chorionic gonadotropin (HCG) and that she was three weeks pregnant."

May speculates, "Is it possible that he stops his work when he finds imperfections on the body that will interfere with his artwork? I mean, he stopped when he was unable to incorporate Brenda McDonald's butterfly into his tattoo and now, he somehow discovers that Matilda Freeman is pregnant, which will distort his work once she starts to show!

"He must also have extensive medical knowledge to be able to sedate his victims for extended periods of time."

Strouse thinks for a moment before answering. "If that's true, we can expect more victims to pop up. Five victims, three of which are confirmed as being the victim of the same perp. Two unconfirmed because we still haven't been able to locate them, but they are likely his first two victims. This shows he's determined to complete his work, what ever that work is!"

One of the detectives reports that his source at the Detroit Free Press is onto the story and he has linked two of the victims, Teresa Malborne and Brenda McDonald. The article is expected to go to print as soon as he gets an interview from one of the victims.

"That might not be all bad." says Strouse. "Perhaps our victims will be more cooperative once their pictures are published. It may also bring other victims to light that will be more willing to show their tattoos."

Strouse continues "there is a theory being floated that the tattoos are meant to tell a story, that the tattoos are interconnected, like chapters in a book. You would need to see all of them to understand the message."

The rest of the team begins to look around, surprised at how this theory materialized considering that no one has even seen one of the tattoos. Who came up with this?

May realizes that she is holding her breath and lets it go once no one asks the question. She hadn't expected Strouse to repeat her theory to the team, especially when there wasn't a shred of evidence to support it. She herself had no idea as to how she had come up with it.

Why had Strouse done that? Was he so desperate, or was he getting ready to throw her under the bus? She comes out of her muse and realized that there are murmurs coming from some of the detectives.

"Ok", says Strouse, "it's only a theory, but it's the only one put forward so far." He realizes he probably shouldn't have mentioned it.

"Detective Manfield did a deep dive on the brother. He died three years ago from a brain hemorrhage. He was a lawyer with McArther, Williams and Zimmerman. I contacted the DA, and he has had the block on Matilda Freeman's records removed. May, you will do the interview as soon as her doctor gives the ok."

Chapter 50

The fury had built up in him. He had to let it out or his mind would literally blow like a gusher, shooting out of the ground higher than the California Fan Palm covering them in black oil, eventually killing them. He needed an outlet, a release. The memory was still so clear.

He had been convicted in a military tribunal fourteen months ago for assault. All he could think about was...how do I get justice for all the things done to me and my people. He stopped sketching, it was hilarious thinking about 'justice' as he sat in this six by eight-foot room. They had plundered his land, taken everything and left only rusted out jack pumps and broken promises.

First came the drilling, night and day, then the tanker trucks would come during the night to empty the tanks located only yards from his house. There was no reason to come at that time, his mother had begged them to change the schedule. Another humiliation. For over ten years he was unable to sleep. Justice. He realizes he is speaking out loud and some of the customers are beginning to take notice. He pays for his coffee but doesn't leave a tip. It tasted almost as bitter as the memories.

Chapter 51

It reads one hundred and fifty-two pounds, that was two pounds over last week. May has never had a problem with her weight. Everyone had expected her to take up a sport that the six-foot height advantage would give her, like basketball or volleyball. But team sports never gave her the thrill that solitary sports like track and field gave her. There was something about breaking a record on your own without the help of others that gave her a sense of euphoria that a team sport never delivered.

Her sport was the pole vault, the feeling she got from running up at full speed and hitting the plant box as she vaulted, using her upper body strength to toss herself into the air, then inverting one hundred eighty degrees while at the same time flipping and arching her back to clear the bar was magical. Her friends couldn't understand that falling almost sixteen feet gave her such pleasure. She would need to try parachuting to see if it gave her the same thrill.

But now pole vaulting would not solve her two pounds, the track would be needed to take care of that. She headed for WSU Athletic Performance Center. *No, why not go to Balduck Park and run the trails?* She had wanted to check out the area where Matilda had been found.

Twenty minutes later she had travelled the six miles to reach her destination, the trail had been steep, and her face had a sheen of perspiration on it. She was thankful for the sixty-degree temperature.

She stopped to check out the surroundings. Mostly brush and the odd poplar tree. She had already viewed it on Google Earth but wanted to get a closer look for herself. There were no structures or caves. No place where he could have kept her for three days. Matilda was in no condition to walk, so he would have needed to carry her. She spotted a trail that could possibly be used by a quad just over a ridge. She walked it for a short distance and found tread marks. Taking out her phone, she made a call to forensics and ordered up a technician to make a cast of the tire. Perhaps it could be used to identify the make and model. She followed the trail, but all tracks disappeared once it went into a grass field.

A thought came to her. Had Brenda not been found in a park? She was pretty sure that Balduck Park was maintained by the city just like Rouge Park was. May had seen the staff use quads to empty trash cans, covering them with a tarp so the refuse would not blow away.

Chapter 52

He had been so careful in choosing the last one. This one progressed further than any of the others before, yet it too had ended in failure, just like the three others before. He flipped through his sketch book, the pages now showing dog ears. It held his master plan, detailing every phase, from the financing right through to the eventual reveal of his art, the work of a genius.

There had been setbacks, but he had anticipated that there would be. Something like this had never been accomplished before, at least not with any success. The plan was solid; he would find another subject and start over.

The one area where a little uncertainty had crept in was the subjects' prerequisites. He had targeted females that had shown interest in art. It was obvious, they would appreciate his work and be enthusiastic about showing it to the world. He had visioned it making headlines on the TV news channels, newspapers and magazines.

He reviewed his notes on his approach to selecting the subject with a pragmatic eye. They had to be Caucasian; the message would show up clearly on white skin. They had to be attractive; he likened it to the framing, a great frame attracts the eye to the picture it holds. No one gives a second look to a book with an ugly cover, and they had to appreciate art. If you don't like the art, you end up putting it in a closet or dumpster. It was this last point that he was beginning to question. Was it enough that they thought the art was beautiful and that it needed to be shown?

Take Brenda McDonald, if he had completed the work, would she, a religious person be enthusiastic about displaying it? He needed someone comfortable in her own skin. To not only be willing to be photographed nude but to embrace it.

What he needed was a model, better yet, an exhibitionist.

Chapter 53

The 737 was at its cruising altitude of thirty-two thousand feet and would arrive at Ronald Reagan Airport a few minutes later. The plane was only one third full. May thought it was a reward for getting up at five thirty in the morning. The seat beside her was empty giving her an opportunity to let her mind meander over the night before when she had dinner with Rob. She began comparing him to Brandon, they were night and day. Brandon had enough testosterone to power the jet she was on. She was definitely attracted to him, but Diane had dropped several hints about her security officer having a roving eye. She knew very little about Rob but what she did know intrigued her. He had been attentive to her, he was good looking, a solid career that he was passionate about and most importantly, he had a good sense of humour.

Her heart began to race. She pulled out her phone and began texting him. *Thank you for the work that you did on deciphering the symbols on the ring. Grandmother looks forward to hearing firsthand what you have discovered and would like to show you her collection, does this weekend work for you?*

Was she moving too fast?

An announcement brought her back. "We will begin descending into Washington in a few minutes, please stow your electronic devices. Thank you for flying Delta."

Her phone beeped. Rob had given her the thumbs up emoji.

Chapter 54

One of the perks of having a father who is high in the upper echelon of Homeland Security is that your vehicle will not be towed, even if it is parked in front of the arrival area at the airport. May spots her dad.

"Thanks for meeting me dad."

"It worked out well. I needed to have a word with Martin Phelps who is in charge of TSA here. You will need to have special clearance for your return trip. The camera can't go through the x-ray machine. How was your flight? Is your mother happy with the paint job?"

"You are in so much doo-doo on that one."

"Really..., I had to get back here, the new administration has turned the whole place upside down! IHOP?" He smiles and leads her to the car.

"So, tell me, how is your investigation going?"

"I'm part of a five-person team dad, and I'm the rookie by far. That said, I'm holding my own and making a difference. Detective Strouse, he is the lead, assigned me to get evidence of the assaults which is why I need the camera. Did mom tell you about my concern about being assigned to this squad?"

"Not much, just that you struggled with the decision, and it was up to you to tell me if you wanted to."

May takes a breath, "Here it is. The administration 'suggested' that I could help by bringing some focus on a pending application for Land Mobile Radio. It's been sitting with HLS for six months and there hasn't been a response."

"Nothing unusual about that. Would you be surprised if I told you that I have had offers ranging from fruit baskets all the way up to memberships at prestigious golf clubs? It has become standard practice to bring focus to proposals. Thank God I haven't received a cake with a dancing girl inside dropped off at my door. Your mother would end me right there! Let me check to see where it sits, and I'll see if I can move it along. What else has been happening in your life?"

"Well, here's something not even mother knows about."

"Oh my, tell me, tell me."

May's eyes brighten, "I met a new man."

"Another cop?"

"No...I mean, it was just the day before yesterday that we met but I really like him. His name is Robert, and he's an associate professor. He's good looking, smart, we share the same interests and most of all, he has a sense of humour."

"That's great, what's his last name?"

"No, you don't, besides I have already done that. He is just fine, thank you, not even a parking ticket."

"You said that you both have the same interest, what is that?"

"He's a semiotician and is interested in the ring grandmother gave me, so he's researching the symbols on it. We'll be going to her house to look through her collection of artifacts and documents to see if we can trace its history."

"Already taking him to see your grandmother. You do know your mother will turn blue if she finds out that your grandmother gets to meet him before she even knows that he exists. She'll probably have a stroke."

She smiles, "I hadn't thought about that. I'll need to think about how to mitigate that. Maybe you should break it to her."

"No thank you. You've already put me in an awkward position by telling me first but it is great news. I hope it works out for you. Let's go pick up the camera. The techs want to demonstrate how to use it and change the film. Then I'll drive you back to the airport and walk you through security. I'll be home on Thursday and can take it back then."

The flight back had even fewer occupied seats, giving her the opportunity to update *The Book*. She noticed there had been an addition that had been entered by one of the other detectives. He had been following up on the quad tracks she had found in Balduck Park. It was identified as a John Deere Crossover Vehicle, commonly known as a Gator. Depending on the model, it could hold up to four people, had four-wheel drive and a cargo bin on the back. Tires matching the tracks were used on this model from 2013 to 2016. Four hundred and ten units were purchased during that time period in the Detroit area. The biggest purchaser by far was the Detroit Parks Dept. They had acquired three hundred and fifteen units. They still operated half of them and sold the rest at auction. A list of employees using them and a list of purchasers was being assembled.

Her phone rang, it was Strouse. "How is the vacation going?"

"If I were on vacation, it wouldn't be in Washington, thank you."

"I wanted to let you know that we've been informed by our public relations officer that the Detroit Free Press will be printing the story. It'll be on the second page tomorrow. Two of the victims have been named along with their pictures taken from an academic yearbook.

"Do we know who the two victims are?"

"We don't have the whole story, but it references abduction and tattooing. It appears that the information came from unnamed sources at the hospital. So, it's reasonable to assume they are Teresa Malborne and Matilda Freeman. It also says that the GAU is handling the case."

"I have the camera with me and will be picking up Brenda tomorrow morning to take her to see Teresa Malborne at Hope Hospital. I have a good feeling that I can at least persuade Brenda to let me see her tattoo and take pictures once she sees the psychological damage this asshole has inflicted on Teresa. Maybe Teresa will let me see her tattoo as well. The fact that the press has gone to print may work in our favour. There's no point in hiding."

"Good luck, I think you're on the right track."

Chapter 55

He has refined his search criteria to include exhibitionists, which was anyone that fell into the area of the performing arts, stage, and fashion model websites. He looked through magazines that advertised nudist resorts, or beaches and swinger parties. He checked to see if there were any burlesque shows performing in the area. He also scoured the internet where photographers and models collaborate like Model Mayhem or PurplePort.

This had reduced the pool of candidates to three possibilities. His training in computer software had paid off in so many ways. He dove deeper into each one, the first had purchased a one-way ticket to France. The second was currently in prison on a fraudulent check charge and wouldn't be out for another month. That left the last one. Linda Spalding, she fit all of the parameters, Caucasian, young, attractive, an aspiring dancer, and based on her Facebook page, quite receptive to having pictures of herself in the nude. Now it was time to see firsthand if the digital image was the same in the real world. He had found that a public persona and what was real could vary greatly.

Chapter 56

May reaches the last page of *The Book,* she has spent the last hour of her flight reviewing it. In the process she has made a summary, calling it her personal profile of the Tattooist. It is definitely crude because she has never taken a profiling course and makes a mental note to do some research on it.

What she knows:

- The perpetrator has extensive medical knowledge
- He has access to sophisticated medical equipment and restricted medication.
- He has experience in instilling fear.
- He is well organized
- He has most likely served time
- He doesn't want his art to be revealed until it is complete.
- Because his art is not complete, there will be more victims.

What she doesn't know:

- What is his motive?
- Why has he risked discovery by not disposing of his victims?

A jolt brings her back from her analysis. She hadn't even heard the announcement that they were about to land.

Chapter 57

Arrangements had been made for herself and Brenda to visit Teresa Malborne at Infinity Hope Center. May picks up Brenda and they had decided to stop at a small diner for breakfast before the appointment time. They had ordered the same, fresh fruit salad and a soft-boiled egg on toast with coffee.

"Brenda, I need to tell you that the Detroit Free Press has discovered that two of the victims where abducted by this creep and what he did to both of you. We don't have names as yet. The story, along with college yearbook pictures will be on the second page this morning. I don't have anymore information about what will be in the article."

Brenda's mouth opens slightly as to speak but says nothing. She picks up her coffee cup and drinks.

A moment passes. "Please tell me what you are thinking."

"I guess…I hoped that it would all just go away. But in reality, it will never go away. I am a walking reminder. I guess that is what he always wanted, a walking reminder."

"Yes, and he's not going to stop, until we stop him."

"I think you're right. It's time to accept that if I ever want to move on."

"There is one other thing I need to tell you before we meet with Teresa. Another victim, a girl about your age, also an art student has been found. She had been reported as missing and we had suspected that she may have been abducted and have been looking for her. Her name is Matilda Freeman, and she is currently in the hospital."

Brenda drops her now empty cup. "Oh my God, I know her. We have attended some of the same classes. Is she going to be all right? I don't know her well, but she seems nice. I have seen her with her boyfriend. They looked happy together."

"She was just transferred out of intensive care. She too was partially covered in tattoos, but like Teresa and yourself, it looks like, for whatever reason he stopped part way through."

"When will this nightmare stop?"

"He won't stop on his own and it's only a matter of time before he abducts another girl or perhaps, he already has. The only way this nightmare will stop is with help from you and Teresa."

Brenda sits silently.

"The answers are in your tattoos. He is telling a story, and he won't stop until it's told. I need to get photographs of both Teresa's and your tattoos. I know that if we put them together it will give the team enough information to catch him. Will you help me stop this monster before he ends up killing the next girl?"

After a long moment Brenda raises her head. "What do you want me to do?"

"Thank you. I have this very special security camera that I borrowed from the FBI. It's very rare and Teresa has heard of it but never seen one. I promised her that I would get it, and she could play with it for an hour or so. The film is impossible to copy, in fact, you can't even see the image without this special filter that you need to lay over the picture. You will each have your own unique filter. The DPD will hold the image. Here, take a picture of me and I'll show you how it works."

May hands her the camera. It is quite large, about half the size of a shoe box. She looks it over and quickly figures out how to operate it. Two minutes later the film is ejected. There is no image, just a white five by five manila strip comes out. May hands her the transparent filter and Brenda lays it over the film. Immediately the color image of May's smiling face appears.

"This is totally secure; you can't buy this camera at any price. What I want you to do is after I show Teresa the camera, I want you to let her take your pictures and then convince her to let you take pictures of her tattoos. Do you think you can do that?"

"I think so. Why do I need to take the pictures, why not you?"

"I will be in the dining area. I don't have the same bond that you two girls have. In some ways, you're sisters now, each of you have a part of something unique. These tattoos are yours and yours alone, not mine and certainly not his. I just need to see them to catch this animal."

"Ok, I understand. I'm willing to have pictures of mine taken but what about Teresa, I mean, she is being treated in a mental health facility because of this. What will it do to her?"

"I have already spoken to Dr. Hamilton, that is who is treating her. I asked exactly that. He told me that it was critical for her to accept her situation. Like any mark on the body, be it a tattoo, birthmark or scar, it was up to the individual whether they showed it or not, but they shouldn't need to fear it."

"That makes sense. I'll do my best. I don't know if she told you but since our talk at the church, I have called her, and we have been texting quite a bit. I think, with this new information, I can get her to help."

Chapter 58

May's phone rings and she makes her apology to the girls. "I'll take this in the dining room. Don't talk about me while I'm gone, this could take a while." She gives them her best smile. The call is from Strouse.

"How's it going?"

"The girls are just getting comfortable with each other. So far, it looks positive."

"Have they seen the paper yet?"

"No but I told Brenda, and she wants to tell Teresa. She thinks it will help build the friendship between them."

"I just got some new information from your old partner Judy Styles. She's been going through old missing persons records and thinks there might be another victim. This one goes back fourteen weeks. Her name is Isabela Steele. She was visiting the Seafoam Palace of Arts and Amusements. Isabela hails from a small town on the northern edge of Lake Huron called Forrester. She was also found in Rouge Park twenty-six hours after her abduction. She didn't show up on the data search because her residence is outside the specified criteria of fifty miles around Detroit."

"She has pulled a disappearing act, probably trying to hide from this creep. Styles is working on tracking her down. She's part of the team now and will be completing a dossier on Isabela as well. Once Judy finds her, she'll give you her location and you can do the interview."

"Ok. I'll come back to the precinct after I drop Brenda back home. I have no idea how long this will take, the longer the better, would be my guess."

Chapter 59

May sits in the dining room with a cup of hot chocolate. Her tablet is open to the Word document that she started on the return flight from Washington and begins to add points.

What she knows:

- The perpetrator has extensive medical knowledge
- He has access to sophisticated medical equipment and restricted medication.
- He has experience in instilling fear.
- He is well organized.
- He has most likely served time.
- He doesn't want his art to be revealed until it is complete.
- Because his art is not complete, there will be more victims.
- He probably learned how to become a tattooist in prison
- He has purchased/stolen a Gator manufactured between 2013 and 2016.

What she doesn't know:

- What is his motive?
- Why has he risked discovery by not disposing of his victims?

May pulls up a list of potential suspects. Strouse had one of the team build the list and it had over twenty-six thousand names. The search parameters had been very broad which included anyone with some level of medical experience, had served time in a penitentiary, had performed tattoos while incarcerated, and is currently released.

She thought she could pare this list down by using some reasonable assumptions.

Let's start with some dates. The first suspected victim was reported almost two years ago. She changes the release date from prison from 2023 to 2021. He would most likely be between the ages of eighteen and fifty. Was it reasonable that a man older would be able to attack six women successfully, transport them, hold them captive, and move them to a park if he where older? Possible, but not likely.

She ran the search. The number of names dropped considerably.

Next, she focused on his medical experience. She removed all names that had not had training as a medic, or experience as a first responder, or took college level courses in medicine for at least one year.

She ran the query again, now we are getting somewhere, the list was down to twenty-two hundred. She took a sip of her chocolate; it was still nice and hot.

"Hi, how was your visit with Teresa?"

May looked up in surprise, the dining room had been empty when she had sat down at the table.

"I'm sorry, my name is Dr. Hamilton, we talked on the phone yesterday. I believe you must be Detective Sheppard?"

"Oh, yes." She taps her tablet to put it into sleep mode and stands up to shake his outstretched hand.

"Please call me May. I only spoke with her for a few minutes. I am waiting for Ms. McDonald to text me before I go back and talk with her. I got the impression they thought I was a mother hen, and they were my chicks, so I left them to chat. Please sit down if you have the time. Have you had a chance to examine Teresa yet? How is she physically?"

He pulls out a chair and does exactly that. "If you are asking if I have seen the tattoos, the answer is no. But what I tried to explain to you on the phone was that for her mental health, it is not important that she shows the tattoo to anyone if she doesn't want to. It's important that she does so, not because she is afraid, but because she wants to do it on her own terms."

"I understand and am in no way applying any pressure. Thank you so much for facilitating this meeting."

"I hope we all benefit from it. Please let me know the results of your meeting."

"I surely will."

Dr. Hamilton stands up to leave and May continues her work on reducing the number of suspects.

Let's look at addresses. Assuming that he lives within twenty miles of Detroit, she runs the list against motor vehicle and parole records for addresses. The list is cut in half. She enters the commands to highlight any names from people that have been contacted during the investigation. No matches found. May's phone beeps, it's a text from Brenda. She saves her query, finishes her chocolate, now cold and heads to Teresa's room with her fingers crossed.

Chapter 60

The girls are sitting side by side on a couch. Brenda's face is expressionless. Teresa's lips are curled into her mouth, what little is showing has turned white. She is looking down at her hands as if she has never seen them before. They hold onto a stack of five-by-five photos.

Teresa raises her eyes to meet May's and looks on. Again, she lowers her eyes at what she holds. Reluctant to move forward, for what? To surrender herself or to be free? May doesn't know.

Should she take the photos from Teresa or wait for her to make the offer? The words of Dr. Hamilton come back. She takes a seat across from them both.

"What did you think of the camera, is it still a myth?"

Her face brightens; this is her comfort zone. She no longer presses her lips together. "I can't believe it, the quality of the image is exquisite in its detail, the colors so vibrant. The ones I took of Brenda's face are truly photorealistic. Every detail is crystal clear and pin sharp. When I first saw it, I thought, this box? It looks so cheap, how can it fulfill its designed purpose as a security camera? Forget that it could actually take any kind of quality picture.

My family attended my graduation which was a big deal. I'm the fifth oldest in a family of eight but the only one to graduate. Some of the kids, richer kids, in my school got cars as graduation gifts, can you believe it. I hadn't expected anything like that, we don't have money. But to my surprise the whole family chipped in and purchased me a gift. It was a Phase One XF IQ4 150MP Camera. It was used but it was the most beautiful thing I had ever seen. The pictures it takes are just amazing. Well, once you've used a camera like mine, you begin to believe that there isn't another one like it.

"Your camera has taken pictures as good, and in some cases even better. Is there a chance I could keep it, just for a few days to show it at school?"

"Not a chance. The FBI was reluctant to even let me have it for one day. I had some very influential people help me get it. You don't want to know how much just the film costs. What you can do is take some pictures of the outside with your cell phone."

May looks over at the bed end table and sees the wrapping of two film boxes. It appears that both sets had been developed.

"What did you think Brenda?"

"It did everything you said it would. We took some of the photos to the reception desk and tried to make copies, they came out white. You kept your word."

Brenda looks at Teresa. Teresa knows it is time to broach the subject.

"Brenda told me that you wanted us to take pictures of the tattoos and use them to find clues to the bastard that did this to us. You have a theory that if we combine the tattoos, join them, there will be a good chance that the DPD will catch him, is that true?"

"That is true, everything so far points to the tattoos. He has chosen different areas to tattoo for each of the victims. Your buttocks Brenda, and Teresa, your front upper body. A third victim has just appeared. Her name is Matilda Freeman and she just came out of ICU. It was her stomach area. The press hasn't found her yet so keep it confidential please. The point is, he's trying to create a picture, and so far has failed to put the entire image on one person because he has found that, what he believes, are imperfections in each of you. Right now, the tattoos are meaningless individually, but put them together like a puzzle, we believe they will provide vital clues, a roadmap to his capture."

Teresa looks at May and says, "I hadn't heard about another victim, will she be all right?"

"She was in really bad shape and is four weeks pregnant, but the doctors think she will survive. We have discovered three other girls about your age that may also have been victims. That makes a total of six. He has no intention of stopping. We need your help to end this madness."

Teresa gives a long look at Brenda and they both nod.

Brenda speaks first, "We did take pictures of each others' tattoos. You're right, individually they are meaningless, but when we put them together, they do appear to form a picture, but there are definitely gaps."

Teresa takes over the conversation. "Together we can make out a group of palm trees, it looks like something is dripping from them. Another appears to be an adobe, the last image is a partial of a tanker truck with part of a name on it."

"Can I see it?"

Brenda says, "We have agreed to show you the pictures, but only you, and just the pictures, not the actual tattoos, for me, it is just too... invasive."

Teresa hands over the stack of pictures and each offers their filters.

May lays the filter over the prints one at a time. "Which one belongs to you Brenda?"

Brenda points to three of the pictures.

May is amazed at the detail of the tattoos. There are three letters on the trailer, an upper case 'T', a lower case 'r', and a lower case 'e'. The back wheels are missing as is the rest of the name. The girls are right about the palm trees, something does appear to be dripping from them. There is a group of three trees. Is it blood, water, no not water, if it was blood, it would be colored red, water, clear. This was black in color. She looks closely at the adobe home. It is a modest unit. Based on the number of windows, she estimates it is a two-bedroom house. It has a brown, wood looking door. On it is the number 23. There is one other item beside the house but is incomplete and she can't make out what it could be.

She puts the pictures down on the table, making sure to keep the filters with the corresponding images.

She had hoped for more, it was no slam dunk, but there was plenty of new data to be researched. She picks up the photos one by one. She needs to sear the images into her brain. There is no telling if she will ever be able to see them again, and the girls where adamant that only she could see them.

"Teresa, we have been trying to understand why this guy seems to have stopped, released his victim and then continues the tattoos on another victim. My theory is that he has found something on each of you that he perceives as an obstacle. Do you have any idea if that would apply to you and if so, what that would be?"

Teresa considers whether she should answer May's question. "I had a breast implant. My left breast was quite a bit smaller than the other. It made me feel lopsided. I couldn't stand it."

"Thank you, girls, this must have been very hard for you. I'll take the pictures as evidence but as we agreed, you hold the filters. It will be up to you if you want anyone else to see them. If you do, just bring your filter to the precinct and ask for Detective Strouse, he'll retrieve the photos from the evidence locker."

"Am I right to say that by meeting each other it has helped you both deal with this horrific event?"

They both nod in agreement.

"Well perhaps meeting Matilda will add to that and help her as well, would you consider meeting her?"

They both smiled and with a resounding voice agreed.

Chapter 61

She was easy to find, she posted countless images of herself on the internet, mostly in the nude. He sat in his white utility van waiting for her to finish her latest gig at *The Big Art* studio posing for a class at $45 per hour. A typical session would last two hours. While she was working, he had gone into the dressing room and retrieved her phone. She didn't even have it locked making it easy to activate the 'find my phone feature'. He took the time to review the article in the Detroit Free Press. He was running out of time. This would be his last chance.

He felt a twinge of guilt, the girls' lives would forever change and probably not for the better. But for the rest of their lives, they would carry a page of his story that had no beginning and no end. He thought of himself as a missionary, the rest of his life was dedicated to exposing the corruption and greed that existed in the company that destroyed his life.

What is his goal? He had spent many days pondering how he could best draw attention to the plight of his people and how *The Monster* had destroyed his life. His sweet mother, his baby sister. As usual, the thought of them brought a wave of despair. The fact that the corporation, Treeman Oil and Gas had gotten away with it, was still getting away with it, drove him into a boiling rage. He had explored just about every avenue to expose them. The media had no interest in his story. Even the local paper had turned him away. The editor made some not-so-subtle suggestions that it was verging on slander, and they would be sued. He quickly realized that asking others for justice was pointless. The people that held power in organizations protected the rich.

The councillor at the penitentiary had tried to tell him different, implying that it was his failure to protect his sister that was the seed he had allowed to grow into a conspiracy. The fool, just another hack, protecting the institutions that believe themselves above the law. He would need to find alternative ways to expose them.

Reading the article, it suggested that they had discovered very few actual facts. The story was mostly about the girls themselves. He knew that the DPD investigation had uncovered a lot more. Again, his computer skills had paid off. He had been able to link to one of the detective's cellphones who had been working at the GAU. Detective Holland had carelessly left his jacket over the back of his chair at the IHOP when he went to the bathroom, probably thinking it was safe because his partner was still eating. Unbeknownst to him, his partner had stepped out to take a call from his boss because it was too noisy in the restaurant. He had positioned himself at the table next to where they had been seated and slipped his hand into the jacket pocket to pull out the phone. It only took twenty seconds to insert the USB drive to link his phone and gain access to all the data. The rest of the data would transfer via Bluetooth so long as he stayed within range. During the time it took to complete their breakfast he had received a wealth of information about the case. He wasn't interested in his picture files, but things like his bank records and calendar could be helpful. Holland had created a group in his contact list containing all the names and phone numbers of the team members. He also had several emails in his sent file referring to something called *The Book*.

He found a text message from someone called Styles. He didn't know much about him/her, but it looked like he/she was a new member of the team. It might be something worth diving into.

A quick call to the DPD Detective Bureau gave him a first name which was enough to find her Facebook page. Surprising how free some people were with their personal information. He had expected that a detective would have more street smarts. He gives a small laugh at his own joke. Along with the usual information, education, career, address, age, he found a lot of interest in dementia, which typically meant that she knew someone close to her had been stricken by the disease.

After this scouting mission was over, he would pay a little visit to 809 Cambridge Street.

Chapter 62

May's grandmother had on her traditional Fon Appliqué: A unique fabric art associated with the Dahomey court, featuring designs that symbolized her family's power and authority. She had on a headwrap of gold and green matching the Fon Applique, a bracelet on her left wrist made of silver that jingled. It was intricately designed and beautifully crafted. On her feet, she had on leather open toed sandals decorated with pearls.

May had called the day before and told her about a new friend she had met who was doing research on the ring. May had wondered if it would be possible for them to view the rest of her collection, in the hopes that it would help him to decipher the symbols that he had not yet identified.

Grandmother, or Nana as she preferred to be called, stood on the steps waiting their arrival. She had been notified of their approach by the security system at the front gate. There had been something in May's voice. This was not going to be a casual tour of her estate by an associate professor with some interest in her heritage, she had known that. This was a hook set by a young detective. She herself was more than just curious as to what her granddaughter was about to reel in.

Rob had insisted on picking her up in his three-year-old Mazda MX-5 Miata. It was a gorgeous day with temperatures in the mid eighties, the sun fully out and he had the convertible top down. May met him at her door. He escorted her to the car and opened the door. Her hair was down and she thought *'this was going to be interesting!'* He went around and opened the trunk while she watched him in the side mirror as he retrieved a red silk scarf and presented it to her.

"This should help keep your hair in place."

With her best smile she says, "thank you" and places the scarf on her head and wraps it around her neck, making sure it won't blow off. She gives him an evaluating look. This is kind of fun, interesting that he has a scarf available. Is this what he does for all the women that he meets?

Oh, stop it! You do this all the time; you discover a man that you like and immediately begin to mistrust him. I do not! *Yes, you do, and you know it! Then you become so suspicious that you drive him away.*

She wakes from her musing when she hears the revving of the engine. He stretches out his arm pointing forward and yells "Tallyho, off we go." Funny, it's a term she has often used.

Nana see a little sports car approach the circular drive and stops in front of her. A man of about thirty hopped out of the car. He has a spring in his step and immediately opened the passenger door offering his hand to assist May's exit. He's wearing brown dress pants, a sports coat with the university logo, over a black light weight turtleneck. His shoes were leather and had been well shined. He was as tall as May with a head of jet-black hair. A fine-looking specimen. Nana is pleased.

Chapter 63

May receives a call from the hospital where Matilda Freeman is being treated. She has recovered somewhat, and the doctor says she is stable enough to be interviewed.

Matilda is in a private room and is sitting up in bed. She is smiling and May suspects she knows why. The nurses have just told her that she is pregnant and that the baby is fine.

"Hello Matilda, I'm detective May Sheppard. I'm one of the six special investigators assigned to work on your case. Thank you for allowing me to meet with you. Has the medical staff told you what has happened?"

"Six investigators working on my case, is that normal?"

"The Detroit Police Department sometimes establishes a special task force when there appears to be a serial attacker involved, it is called The General Assignment Unit or GAU. We are taking this case very seriously. Are you ok to tell me what happened?"

"I don't remember much. I was walking to my car after taking my last class and I felt this sharp pain in my neck."

"We believe your assailant used a taser to knock you out. The doctor found burn marks on your neck. What time was this and where was your car parked?"

"It was getting late and it was already dark, maybe nine PM. I had to park a long way from the Arts building at Wayne because I got there late. It was at the far end of section E."

May makes a note to see if there are any cameras in that section of the parking lot.

She nods for her to continue.

"After that, everything is hazy, I remember pain on my stomach and there is a bright light shining in my eyes. There was someone looking down on me. I can't make out a face.

"I finally wake up from this dream and it turned into a nightmare. My stomach really hurts now, its burning. I can't close my eyes. I can't even blink. Its as if they have been taped open. There is a TV hanging from the ceiling. Screams are coming from the speakers. It's horrible, I don't want to talk about it."

"It's ok. It has happened to several other girls and we have a good idea what this monster did to you. Do you remember anything else, how he looked or sounded?"

"He told me that I was pregnant. I don't know how he found out, but the doctor just confirmed it."

"In some ways you are fortunate. If he hadn't discovered that you were pregnant, we believe that he would have continued until he covered your whole body."

"I'm afraid I don't know what my fiancée will do when he sees what that creep has done to me but I think he will be happy about the baby, he loves kids."

"I've spoken with him and he seems like a very strong, nice young man. I called him a few minutes ago and he's on his way."

"Does he know what this guy did to me, about the tattoos I mean?"

"I want to talk to you about that. There have been five other attacks. All the victims have been tattooed and each one appears to be different but they are of the same picture. We have made great progress in putting the pieces together. We believe that if we add yours, it will give us enough information to stop him before he abducts his next victim. Would it be ok if I looked at yours?"

"He's a monster. He promised me that if I showed it to anyone, he would skin me alive. He knows where I live, my school, even where I work part time."

"We know and you're right, he is a monster and one we must stop. The other girls went through the same thing. They too were threatened, but we made a deal with them. Do you want to hear it?"

May tells her about the camera and all the security features it has. "If you like, you can meet two of the girls and they can confirm it. They are in the cafeteria waiting for my call. They really want to help. Should I call them?"

"I guess it wouldn't hurt to talk with them."

"I'll call them right now."

It took a few minutes for the girls to appear. May was waiting for them in the hall. She hands Teresa the camera and leads them into the room.

"Matilda Freeman, this is Brenda McDonald and Teresa Malborne, these are the girls I was telling you about. I need to go and update my boss so why don't you get to know each other, and I'll be back in a bit."

May is about to hit the speed dial for Strouse, but just before she does, she looks back at the room where she can hear the girls talking.

Have I stepped over the line? What will he say when I tell him that I involved the girls to this extent? She definitely got the results she was hoping for and if anything, it had been beneficial for both Brenda's and Teresa's mental state. As far as she knew it had been the right thing to do, she had not put them in danger and had accomplished her assignment.

May pressed the button, perhaps she didn't need to get into the weeds unless he asks.

Chapter 64

May waits for Brenda's text and uses the time to review the new information that the photographs produced. Its all from memory now but the images are clear in her mind. On her phone she pulls up images of palm trees. She has never seen one in real life. Her mind drifts, how is it that she has been so... sheltered? No, it has been her choice. She had plenty of opportunity to wander the world, she was just never interested. There had been only one trip abroad and that was with her Nana to west Africa. She has not even been south of the 37th parallel in her own country.

She is immediately disappointed in her search results. Wikipedia shows that there are around 2,600 species of palm trees. She makes another assumption. Her jaws clench, she hates making assumptions because they will almost always lead you down the wrong path, but if it's framed right, the risks can be mitigated, and she had to narrow the search parameters. All of the victims had said he didn't have an accent. So, wasn't it reasonable to assume he was American? She changes the search to show only palm trees that grow in the United States. She types and is delighted with the results.

The United States is home to 14 native palm tree species, belonging to 9 genera. These palms are primarily found in the southeastern and southern states, such as Florida, Texas, and parts of California. Additionally, two species—the coconut palm and the date palm—have become naturalized in certain areas. Florida boasts the highest diversity of palm species, while the California fan palm is the only palm native to the western United States.

She brings up a picture of the California fan palm. *Well, that sure looks like the palm in the tattoo. That along with the adobe house sure pointed to California.*

May gets a notification on her phone from Brenda. Ok, lets see if my amateur detectives were able to come through for me. As she approaches Matilda's room, she spots a young man in the waiting area and approaches him.

"Hi, I'm detective Sheppard, are you Matilda's fiancée? We spoke on the phone a few hours ago."

"Yes, thanks for your call. I had been told by someone at the nursing station to wait here while the police interviewed her about the attack."

"We're almost finished. Can you give us a few more minutes? She's an amazing woman. You are very lucky."

"Yes and thank you."

May walks into the room and sees three smiling faces. Matilda is holding a stack of pictures.

Chapter 65

Strouse calls for an early morning meeting and everyone met in the conference room promptly at seven AM.

"Ok, people we are making headway. May, give us a description of the tattoos you have seen thus far."

May stands, "We have obtained photographs of the tattoos from three of the victims, Brenda, Teresa and Matilda. Unfortunately, you will not be able to view them yourselves at this time, as the victims won't permit it, and they have exclusive rights to them. They did give me an opportunity to look at them. When we put them together it shows a group of three palm trees, there appears to be oil dripping from the fronds, and a small adobe house with the number 23 on a wooden door. There is also a tanker truck with the name Treeman Oil and Gas on the side. What looks like a jack pump is visible near the house and next to it is a cross with the name Sandy and the date Aug. 13, 2014. The last tattoo is a symbol that we haven't identified yet."

Strouse takes over, "If we continue on with the hypothesis that the tattoos are a road map to catching this guy, we can begin narrowing our search. Start focusing on California and New Mexico. Create a new list of candidates that have served time in those states who have medical training, tattooing skills and are no longer incarcerated. Interview their cellmates and staff. Find out if there are any connections to this company called Treeman Oil and Gas."

"May, Styles, you'll fly down and meet with Mr. Jesus R. Hernandez, he is the CEO of Treeman Oil and Gas. Here's his address and he's expecting you. Find out who has issues with him and his company."

Chapter 66

Styles insists on driving to the airport. They are on standby for a 11:32 flight that morning into McClellan-Palomar Airport. It's just past nine, but they want to be first on the list.

May's eyes drift to the side mirror for the third time. Over the last four miles or so, she has noticed that same car. She makes a note of the plate number and description. Styles spots what she's doing and glances in the rear-view mirror.

"You think he is following?"

"For at least four miles, I think we should stop and have a chat."

Styles suggests, "Lets call it in and have a patrol car pull them over, it's probably just a reporter and I don't want to be bumped off this flight."

May takes out her phone and calls dispatch, gives her badge number and location as well as their destination. "We need a patrol car to pull over a late model dark blue Palisade, with Michigan licence number LLS954. Have them get driver ID and report back to us before letting go."

They drive for another ten minutes before May tells Styles that she sees the red and blues pulling over the Palisade.

Shortly after, May's cellphone rings. "You were right, the car is registered to the same woman that wrote the story on our victims."

Style responds with "at least we lost her, she won't know where we're heading."

Strouse had already cleared the way with Transportation Security Administration (TSA) so that they could carry their weapons on the plane. They passed security without any issues and proceeded to the boarding area. There was only about 15 people seated. Styles was chatting up the attendant, flashing her badge like it was a golden ticket to paradise and giving the young agent her best smile.

May used her time for more personal reasons. "Good morning. Are you teaching a class? I can call back."

"Good morning to you, just marking some exams."

"I have a favour to ask you, well it's actually for the DPD."

"Oh, I understand that they hand out 'get out of jail' cards to citizens that help them in their investigations."

"Don't you wish. I have discovered a tattoo that looks like a symbol of some kind. If I describe it to you, could you point me in the right direction where I might find more details about it."

"Well, if I can't get a 'get out of jail' card, perhaps there could be some other kind of reward for my services."

"What are you thinking would be a fair trade?"

"How about a date this Saturday? *Les Misérable* is performing at the Stranahan Theater, and I can get tickets."

"Well...let's see how you do from your end."

"Ok, send me the image."

"That's the thing, I don't have it, I can only describe it to you. It is a circle that has been divided into four quadrants, each quadrant has the image of an animal. The top left is that of a horse, to the right a bison, under it, a bird-of-pray and to the left of the bird is a fox or wolf. The whole thing sits in what could be a basket."

"That sounds interesting, can you draw it out for me?'

"I'm a terrible artist, but let me give it a try, you should have something in about an hour. I'm on a flight to San Diego but I can get it to you before the flight leaves."

"I look forward to it."

Rob tilts back in his chair, tapping the end of the pencil to his lower lip and looks at the ceiling. He has a pretty good idea what she is describing.

May heads for the bar, orders orange juice and grabs a napkin. Two attempts later she has a reasonable depiction of the tattoo she saw in the picture. She adds arrows to some areas and indicates the colors of the lines. She only has a blue ink pen. She pulls out her phone, takes a picture and sends it to Rob.

Styles comes and sits beside her. "We are first on the wait list."

"Good, did you have any luck locating Isabel Steele?"

"Last known to have flown to Mexico four weeks ago, no trace of her since. She hasn't used her credit cards or her phone."

The flight arrives five hours and ten minutes later in an overcast sky. They rent a car at the airport and drive fifteen minutes to downtown and check into the Hilton Hotel. Treeman Oil and Gas is located on the eighteenth-floor next door. They had an appointment to meet with Mr. Hernandez the next morning at nine.

"May, have you ever been to San Diego before?"

"No, I haven't travelled much."

"Well, I'm very familiar with this city. Would you like me to show you the town? We can have dinner at Seaport Village and tour Balboa Park and SeaWorld San Diego."

"Sounds great, let me change and I'll meet you in the lobby in about an hour."

Styles sits at the bar where she can see the lobby and orders a gin and tonic when her phone rings. The display shows 'unknown caller.'

"Hello?"

"Detective Judy Styles, how nice to finally talk with you."

"Who is this?"

"My name is of no concern, but I can help you with your problem, your financial problem that is. Your father needs better care than he's getting, and you can't afford to move him to a better facility. So, I am offering you a lifeline. How does fifty thousand dollars for each of the next three weeks sound to you?"

"That sounds to good to be true. What would you expect from me, and how did you get this information?"

"I broke into your apartment. I'm surprised that you left a booklet with all your passwords right beside your computer, tisk, tisk. You are behind in your personal loans. Did you borrow the money to pay for your father's medical bills? They are sure adding up. Are you not required to disclose financial hardships to Internal Affairs? As for what I want is time. Time to complete my work. You only need to make sure that the GAU doesn't interfere with it for the next three weeks. A little misdirection, a heads up. That's all, and for that I will give you the fifty grand every week for the next three weeks. No one will know and no one will get hurt, but most of all, your father, the man you owe everything to will have the care he disserves."

Judy squeezes the phone harder and harder thinking 'that son of a bitch, he wants to make this personal. Fine, I can make it personal.'

"What do you hope to accomplish in the next three weeks? How many more girls' lives will you destroy? Tell me what this is all about."

"Judy, haven't you figured it out yet? I thought my work would have given you enough information by now. Perhaps I have overestimated the DPD. The offer is good until tomorrow at eight AM sharp. I will call you back at that time for your answer. Good night, Judy."

Chapter 67

Commander Ji-An was on the phone and the receiver was getting warm as she held it to her ear when she heard a ping coming from her computer. It announced that she had another e-mail. It was nine-fifteen in the morning, and it had gone off six times already. She tried to imagine how many had actually been addressed to her but she knew her assistant was weeding out four or five for every one she got.

She glanced at the title from Homeland Security/Purchasing Department.

"OK I'll get back to you on that" and puts the phone back in the receiver.

She opened the e-mail and read the subject line.

Your grant application for the Hexagon Safety & Infrastructure's Intergraph Artificial Intelligent (AI) Computer Assisted Dispatch I(CAD) has been approved.

Your purchase order is P49W-621.

Sincerely.

Mrs. Zofia Wiśniewski

Director of Purchasing, Homeland Security

She gets up from her chair and with a strong voice says "Thema!"

Thema Eastman, Ji-An's longtime assistant, is already standing in the door frame. "Is this real?"

"I just got off the phone with Homeland and the purchase order is valid."

"For how much?"

"Are you ready for this? The full amount!"

"I can't believe it. I had expected, if we got approval, it would only cover eighty percent of the project. This is fantastic."

Thema continues, "Have you read the attachment?"

Ji-An looks back at her display, sees the icon and proceeds to click on it.

It is a letter addressed to her.

Congratulations on your successful submission for the new communication system. It will be a vital tool to fight against the threat of terrorism, as well as aide your officers in their day to day duties protecting the citizens of Detroit.

The Hexagon Communication System that you have chosen has been requested by other police departments of your size (Phoenix Police Department and Philadelphia Police Department).

In both cases the implementation stumbled because insufficient resources were not committed at the onset of the project. I strongly recommend that you submit a supplemental request for the following resources to achieve a successful transition to the new system.

Homeland Security recommends the following additional resources be added to your plan:

1 - Special Project Manager, eight-month term assignment

1 - Software engineer to set up the AI specifications and migrate the data bases – one year term

1 - Training instructor, 4 to 6 months

2 - Technical installers (one for the mobile units and one for the head end unit), 6 months

The estimated cost to implement a project of this scale is $350,000.

Homeland will be receptive to your submission to cover the cost of these vital resources.

Sincerely.

Martin Sheppard, Director
Office for State and Local Law Enforcement
Homeland Security

Ji-An looks up at Thema.

"I have already created a supplemental file for the project under the current folder. I'm in the process of contacting Hexagon Communication to obtain budget quotes for the recommended resources and finding additional companies that meet the requirements. I should be able to submit RFPs for your approval by end of week."

Thema hears her phone ring and hurries back to her desk. She calls to Ji-An, "Its Homeland calling." She clicks for the call to go through.

"Commander Ji-An, this is Martin Sheppard. I just wanted to congratulate you personally on your successful submission."

"Hello, Director...thank you so much."

"Normally I would come out and be there for the public announcement in person, but in this case, I will have my deputy take that role. So, please don't hesitate to call him directly if you need anything. Again congratulations. Perhaps we can meet in the near future to discuss how Homeland Security can assist the DPD further. Goodbye."

She thinks, *not a man interested in pleasantries.*

She picks up the phone. "Darius, got plans for lunch?"

Chapter 68

May and Judy met on the main floor which offered the courtesy breakfast for all hotel guests. Last night they had exceeded the seventy four dollar per diam expense permitted by the DPD. Seaport Village was in the tourist district, and they charged tourist prices, even to cops, Judy had asked.

Over coffee Judy says, "I called Strouse late last night and told him about the call."

"What did he say?"

"He's sending a forensic team to my apartment. I had to notify the landlord to let them in. He wants to cover all the bases, but I think the perp is too smart to have left anything behind. Strouse is having my phone set up for a trace but we both think it'll be a waste of time."

She takes a sip of her coffee "Strouse is concerned though and he may be forced to pull me off the team. He's required to inform Internal Affairs and they might say that I'm compromised, but for now, I stay on the case."

"I'm sorry this has exposed you. I know you're a private person and this is nobody's business but your own."

Judy's phone rings. She looks at May and says, "He is prompt, it's eight o'clock on the nose."

"Good morning detective, have you made a decision?"

"I have. I want a hundred thousand in cash up front for the first two weeks and fifty thousand for each week thereafter or its no deal."

He pauses, but only for a moment "I think I can work with that. Give me a day to collect the money. I'll text you where you can pick it up."

The line goes dead.

May says "He doesn't seem to have a cash flow problem."

"It's time, let's go."

"Good morning, Detectives Styles, Sheppard, what can I do for you?"

Mr. Hernandez stood to receive them and offered them a seat.

"Thank you for meeting with us." May responded. "We're here because your company's name came up during an abduction investigation by the DPD."

"That happened two years ago, did you find the person or persons involved? Mr. Treeman will be so relieved."

Judy gives May a confused look.

Judy says, "Our case is more recent than that. What case are you referring to?"

"It was before I arrived at Treeman Oil and Gas but I can tell you that it was his daughter that was taken. Fortunately, he paid the ransom, and the kidnapper or kidnappers released her unharmed. They were never apprehended. You would need to contact Mr. Treeman directly. If you want further details, my assistant can give you his address and phone number. His family lives in the Rancho Santa Fe district."

"We'll do that, thank you", says May. "Our investigation is more current and it involves a tanker truck with the name Treeman Oil and Gas on it. What can you tell us about it?"

"Mr. Treeman brought me in because of my experience in dealing with the abundance of insurance claims the company has had to file. There have been over 32 serious cases of vandalism reported, costing the company two point two million dollars.

"We have one hundred and forty-two oil tanker trucks, but none of them carry the Treeman name any longer. I had the names removed hoping it would stop the vandalism."

"How long ago did you remove the name from your trucks?"

"It was soon after I arrived. It was obvious to me that we were being targeted because it was only happening to trucks and equipment that had our name on it. The vandalism stopped soon afterwards."

"Just one more question, what areas do your trucks cover?"

"We service over eighteen hundred oil and gas fields all over California and New Mexico and we are expanding west and north from there. I can give you a digital map that will help pin our wells if you like."

"Thank you that would be helpful."

Chapter 69

Rancho Santa Fe is a residential community of about 1,400 households. Notable residents include Bill Gates, Phil Mickelson and John Moores to name just a few. May had called ahead to see if Mr. Treeman was available. His secretary said he was and would meet them at 11:30. They couldn't see the house as they drove down the winding driveway. A tall stone wall surrounded the estate. A guard house stood next to a black iron gate. Two men approached their car, one from ether side.

"Good morning, ladies, may I see some identification please?" He took the ID's to the guard house while the second guard looked in and around the vehicle. May noticed that he took a picture of the licence plate and the car.

"Can you please open the trunk Ma'am?"

Judy obliged. "Pretty heavy security."

It took three minutes before the first guard returned with their ID's and issued them security badges.

"Please stay on the main drive. You'll see the Chamber House in about 500 yards past the tree line. The valet will park your vehicle for you and the house manager, Mr. Timmons will meet you at the door."

The heavy gate opened outward, and they drove ahead. May pointed to the tree line where an armed guard was holding a leashed dog. She spotted two more before they saw the house.

The place was huge and it deserved its own name. It was constructed of limestone following the architectural style of a British manor house. Mr. Timmons greeted them warmly and guided them through the reception room to the elevator. The inside was ultra modern, in stark contrast to its exterior. May noticed extensive security measures had been added. "How long has Mr. Treeman lived here?"

"Construction of Chamber House was started almost two years ago. Mr. Treeman, his daughter, Trudy, and Mrs. Treeman moved in immediately upon its completion two months ago." Mr. Treeman is in his office; he'll meet with you there."

"Thank you for meeting with us on such short notice Mr. Treeman," said Judy.

"Of course. You mentioned there might be a development in my daughter's abduction case?"

"Possibly." May takes over the questioning. "What actually brought us here is related to several abduction cases that occurred in Detroit. Some information was found linking your company to those cases. When we spoke to Mr. Hernandez, he informed us that your daughter had been abducted two years ago. Obviously, we want to see if this could also have a connection. Would you be able to give us the details?"

"Mr. Hernandez called me earlier and told me about your inquiries. My daughter, Trudy, was abducted while at summer camp just over two years ago. She was just twelve years old. A man called me at my home, we lived in Palm Springs at the time, demanding one point five million dollars in small denominations.

"He made horrible threats about what he would do to her if I contacted the police. It made me sick. He told me to bring the money to the desert by noon the following day. I did as he instructed, but he never showed. It was three days of hell before he called back. Again, he made me drive to the desert, this time there would be written instructions about where to place the money. He hung up before I could ask about Trudy. I did as I was instructed. I left the money and drove home. Trudy called three hours later. She had not been physically harmed. She remembers almost nothing. The police took blood samples and they determined that she had been drugged. The incident has turned our lives upside down. We moved into this ... fortress, hired a small army of guards. She is afraid to go to school so now we have a private tutor come here. The fear of her being abducted again is tearing this family apart.

"If there is anything you can do to catch this monster, I will be eternally grateful. If you need more information, you can contact Special Agent Tom Billings at the FBI. He's stationed in San Diego."

May asks "Did the abductor leave any kind of marks on your daughter?"

"Marks?"

"Yes, a tattoo for example."

"Oh, heavens no, a mark like that... a permanent reminder, my God!"

"Thank you, Mr. Treeman, we will contact agent Billings" says Judy.

Chapter 70

Judy drives back to San Diego while May updates Strouse on the latest developments.

"Now that's interesting" says Strouse. "If we contact the FBI there is a reasonable probability that Special Agent Billings and the FBI will take over the case."

"Yes, but if we don't, what will happen when Mr. Treeman calls Billings for an update? You can be sure he will, and then Billings will find out that we've been holding out on him."

"Ok, here's what you'll do. Call the FBI field office in San Diego and leave a message for Agent Billings to call you. Don't talk with him directly. When they ask who you are, give only your first name and change one digit in your call back number. Use a burner phone to make the call. We can honestly say we tried to call him and give him an update, but it's not our fault if he doesn't call back."

"You are a devious bastard."

"Not my first rodeo. Good work ladies. Ji-An came by wanting to know where you were. She seemed to be in a good mood though, so I don't think you're in trouble. Anything I should know about?"

May thinks for a moment...perhaps too long a moment. "No, nothing I can think of."

"Ok then."

May had only a few seconds to think about it before her phone rang. "Hi, got a sec?"

It was Rob, "Sure, what's up?"

"I have some information about the picture you sent me. I had it enlarged and framed and now it's hanging where the Mona Lisa used to be."

She smiles into the phone. "Very funny. Mock my artwork one more time and I'll hang you on a wall!"

"I think I'm going to collect on that date. What you drew is a variation on the Jicarilla Apache Nation emblem. I looked it up on Google. The Reservation covers approximately one million acres in north-central New Mexico on the eastern edge of the San Juan Basin, comprising parts of townships 22 to 32 north and ranges 1 east to 5 west. Is that helpful?"

May thinks for a minute, "I think you should get those tickets for this Saturday before they're gone."

A victorious 'yes' blasts from the phone.

"I'll pick you up at three and we can do dinner afterwards" he hangs up before she can answer.

She smiles, thinking, *'this is turning out to be a pretty good day.'*

May calls Strouse. He picks up and says, "You again." From the tone of his voice, she can tell he's joking. "If you have a moment, can you do a search for me? We are in the car and the screen is too small."

"Ok, shoot."

"Look for a death certificate for a Sandy that died on August 13th, 2014."

"We did that already, came up with thirty-six names."

"Yes, but this time, change the geological area to the Jicarilla Apache Nation Reservation."

"I got one hit. A Sandy River, she was eight when she died."

"Does the death certificate have her address on it? Does it have the house number as twenty-three?"

"Holy shit! I'm going to look for the obituary in the local paper. I'll get back to you ASAP."

Judy gets a call from Captain Jackson, her immediate supervisor. "Hello Judy, just want you to rest easy, the IA folks cleared you to keep working on the case."

"Thanks Captain, that's good to know."

An hour later the girls are having lunch. Judy recommended eating at a food truck called Kiko's Seafood Place. They both chose Fish Tacos. She says it is a true San Diego classic, often served Baja-style with battered and fried white fish, cabbage, crema, and salsa. Food trucks are known for their delicious fish tacos.

May's phone rings, "You're onto something. I found her obituary in the weekly tribal newsletter. It's short, says she died accidentally but doesn't say how. She is survived by her brother, Mathew River and her mother. His name comes up in the list of persons that served time. I have tried to get hold of the editor but was told he is out hunting and won't be back for several days. The death certificate has an address of 23 Baishan Way, Goyathlay New Mexico. It is on the Jicarilla Apache Nation Reservation. We have a Mathew River who enlisted in the marines at 18 years of age and trained for two years as a medic. He served eighteen months in the Marine Corps Brig, Camp Pendleton in California when he was charged and convicted for theft of narcotics. While incarcerated he registered for a course in computer science in which he excelled. He was released on June 13, 2022. We lost track of him after that.

Send Judy back here, she needs to pick up her hundred thousand. You go to the village and interview anyone that will talk about what happened back on Aug. 13th 2014. Goyathlay has only one hundred and seventy-five residents according to the 2020 census. Check in with the Tribal Authority first, they have jurisdiction. Tread lightly, we don't want to explain why we were on a reservation to the FBI. I will send you a text with the obituary and anything else we find."

May looks up the best way to get to the reservation. Her Map app shows it as a thirteen-hour drive. Her only option is to get a flight to Albuquerque, rent a car and stay overnight. Then get a fresh start in the morning for a two-and-a-half-hour drive to the reservation.

May passes on the information to Judy. "Let's drive to the hotel and check out, see if we can get flights."

On the drive to the airport Judy asks, "Do you think it's the same guy?"

"Looks that way to me. I mean we can't get tunnel vision, but the arrows are all pointing in the same direction. The timelines sure seem to fit. He gets released from prison, probably where he learned how to tattoo. He gets out and the vandalism starts. Then he abducts Mr. and Mrs. Treeman's daughter. The vandalism stops. Shortly afterwards he starts abducting girls in Detroit. Sure, there are some gaps, like, why is he focused on Treeman and his company?"

"He must feel that they have wronged him somehow" says Judy.

"He has already gotten his revenge by kidnapping Treeman's daughter and putting him and his family into a self-imposed gilded prison. He has also gotten away with a small fortune.

"What is his goal? Why is he attacking girls in Detroit? We haven't found any connection to Treeman and those girls."

"That's a good question" says May.

May thinks about it and says "maybe the girls are incidental to his plan, just a means to an end. Let's go back to the premise that the tattoos are his story. Most people tell a story in one of three ways. They write it, in a book or magazine, etc. They can use audio media like records, podcasts, radio or even a song.

The third way is through the visual arts. Photographs, video or perhaps something more.....unique?

Judy follows her train of thought. "Tattoos!" But once he has completed his story, how does he get it out there? What is the point of recording a story if no one gets to see it?"

May thinks, "He must have a plan to do just that. He's smart and he wouldn't go through all this without one. Perhaps he'll send photographs to the papers or maybe he's hoping for a big media trial."

Chapter 71

He had spent half the night looking for the right location. Cameras and microphones had been installed inside and outside of the old panel van. He had sewn a tracker into the fiber handle of the sports bag that held the money and had driven to Edgewater Park. The amusement park had been abandoned many years ago. He was confident that it had no cameras in the parking lot, and it was easy for him to gain access.

Once the van had been parked, he flattened the tires so it couldn't be stolen and locked the doors. He then took out the burner phone and texted the location to detective Styles.

She would have one hour to get to the site and pick up the money. There was a high degree of concern that she would betray him. He suspected that the DPD would go to the site of the truck and surveil it from a distance, hoping that he would come to retrieve the money if Styles did not show up. To avoid losing the money, he had placed the bag holding the money in an old wooden box used to hold traction sand just at the edge of the parking lot. One of the cameras hidden on the van had clear site of the box. He had covered the bag with some of the sand so that it was not visible. It could stay there without the risk of being found for months. If she did show up and it appeared that she was alone, he would call her and tell her where the money was.

The whole thing had taken more time and resources than he had expected. It had not been part of the plan. He now wondered if he had made a mistake. They were getting close to discovering who he was. The bug he had placed in the GAU conference room was paying off. He was not too concerned about losing the money, he had enough to meet his goals. Time was the problem. He had underestimated how long it would take to find the right subject matter to publish his message. One, perhaps two girls would do, not six. If she slowed the investigation by misdirecting the GAU a week or two, this risky maneuver would be worth it.

He looked over his timeline on his tablet. He had placed data points for expenses on the vertical and milestones on the horizontal. The black line on the graph showed the predicted progress, the red line tracked the reality. He had to speed up or they would identify him and make the anticipated arrest before he had all of the plan in place.

He reviewed his current expenditures to date. The one million five-hundred thousand payment by Mr. Treeman would easily cover all of the expenses.

Thirty-foot Cuddy Rental from Ship Rentals out of San Diego, three days at $3,000 per day. He had kept Trudy Treeman on the boat, moving to different remote anchor points every day. He had thought about tattooing his sister's obituary on her arm, but she was so young, and he was not out to punish her, but her father and his company.

Travel and accommodation over the last two years. Again, moving every year from a townhouse to an apartment to finally a farmhouse just outside of Detroit, $120,000.

Medical equipment, electronics and vehicles, $85,000.

Payments to DPD, $100,000.

His future costs were budgeted as well. Hiring a professional model photographer, one that was morally compromised, $10,000.

Billboards for a one-month term in every state of America, with special focus on New Mexico and California, $62,000.

He had reserved a full-page advertisement in three of the most popular arts magazines; Average cost, $7,000 each. Her picture would be the topic of every conversation. He had orchestrated it to be a blitz. And let's not forget the pound of flesh for the blood sucking lawyers who will defend him at the trial. He had no idea as to how much that would come to so he put in $90,000.

That brought the total to approximately $497,000.

He had already prepared multiple video confessions to his acts, carefully explaining why he had carried them out. His manifesto detailed the brutality of what Mr. Treeman and his company Treeman Oil and Gas had done to his family. Not just the criminal act, but also how he used his money and influence to perverse the so-called justice system. He also pointed the finger at the Treaty Police Department and the FBI for their incompetence investigating his sister's death, ruling it an accident. There was one other entity that was highlighted, the band council. It was the same story all over the world. He had seen it while serving in Iraq where if you didn't belong to the ruling clan, you would be marginalized at best. It was the same on the reserve. His family was on the wrong side.

Chapter 72

The GPS said it was a three-hour drive from Albuquerque to Dulce, New Mexico where the Jicarilla Apache Police has its office. May left the hotel at nine AM to arrive just in time to invite Mr. Vincent Altaha, the investigator that filed the report into the death of young Sandy River, for lunch. She hoped that a relaxing atmosphere over a meal would quell the usual suspicions when one police department makes inquiries into another's case. If not handled correctly it could appear to some as if they are looking over their shoulder.

The Jicarilla Apache Nation Reservation has a population of approximately 3,176 people. It spans 1,316 square miles. The Jicarilla Apache Police Department employs 23 officers. Vincent was a junior detective with four years of experience.

They had agreed to meet at the local watering hole near the precinct building. On the drive down May had wondered what he would be like. Thoughts of western attire came to mind, cowboy boots, six gun and an old cowboy hat. *"Let's go through a little racial profiling and add a feather in the cap, why don't you",* says the voice in the back of her head.

When she first walked in, she scanned the room, it was at half capacity. She tried in vane to pick out a likely candidate but just about every male had a side arm. Some openly visible, some showed a bulge under a jacket. This was a different world. It was getting a little awkward standing just inside the door, so she chose a small booth in a corner and waited to be approached. She checked her phone and saw she was ten minutes early. A waitress appeared and set down a glass of water.

"Would you like a cup of coffee while you wait for Detective Altaha, Detective Sheppard?" Wow, May wondered if she had left her name tag and badge on.

"Vincent is just running a little late. He called me and said you would be coming. Oh, there is his car pulling up now."

He was dressed in a casual summer business suit no tie, but he did have cowboy boots. He was a good looking man of about thirty five years of age. Definitely had a native ancestry.

"Detective Sheppard, welcome to Jicarilla Apache Nation."

"Thank you, please call me May"... interesting, not welcome to New Mexico or Dulce. First sign was that he believed this was his native land and that she was a guest here.

Before he even sat down the waitress was back with two cups filled with coffee. "The usual?"

"Sure" said Vincent as he sat down, she was off without another word.

"All the way from Detroit, must be important."

May fixes her coffee trying to slow the pace, hoping to get a sense of the man. So much for her strategy of having a relaxing lunch.

"I am trying to get some facts on the death of a Sandy River."

"You mentioned that in your text message. Why is she of interest to the DPD?"

"We're investigating multiple abductions that we believe are linked to her death."

"I see, your primary suspect is Mathew River."

May shows surprise. "He is a person of interest in this investigation. How did you jump to that conclusion?"

He gives her a long look, tilts his head to the ceiling. "We are both police officers and you didn't come all this way to play games. Can you show me a little courtesy and be frank?"

May is taken aback. She remembers Strouse's warning. "He is our only suspect. Six Caucasian girls have been abducted, some held for only a few hours, some as long as four days. He tattoos each of them. We believe the tattoos are telling his story. So far there isn't a complete picture, just a piece of the picture on each of the girls. I believe he's trying to put them all together on one person. So that means there will be at least one more victim. I can't show you any of the tattoos because all the victims have been scared out of their minds and won't let us photograph them. But I have seen them. Every one of them points to this reserve. His house number, 23. A crest, closely matching common Apache symbols. The name of Treeman Oil and Gas company on a tanker truck and the name Sandy on a cross. I believe he was also involved in the abduction of Treeman's daughter's kidnapping two years ago."

The waitress arrives with their lunch. There are multiple dishes taking up most of the table. She recognizes most of them. There is a plate with six enchiladas, a huge bowl of Mexican rice and two small hamburgers, she thinks they are called sliders, but there are two dishes that she has never seen before. Everything smells great and is steaming hot.

May looks closely at each dish. There is enough food to feed a family of six. He begins placing some of the food on his plate then stops. She is looking at him like a deer in the headlights.

He uses his fork as a pointer naming each dish in turn. "Green Chile Cheeseburger, Enchiladas, Posole, a kind of stew made with hominy, pork, and red or green Chile, Sopaipillas, a puffy fried bread served with honey, and my favorite, Chiles Rellenos which are roasted green chiles stuffed with cheese, battered, and fried." He continues to pile the food onto his plate. She follows suit. "I would go lightly on the Posole if you are planning to drive back to Albuquerque today. After lunch I'll take you to his home and show you the property. I have a copy of the file in the car that you can have."

They left the restaurant forty minutes later. He insisted on paying the bill and May noticed he didn't leave a tip. She thought about doing so but it might be considered an insult, so she wrote a thank you note and left it on the table.

They arrived twenty minutes later. There was a stark difference from the east side of town as you moved west. The houses where getting smaller, the yards less kept and the road was rough. They pulled into the driveway and approached the house from the back door. She had seen the number 23 on the front. She was surprised when he didn't knock but instead used a key to unlock it. He placed the file on the living room table and opened it to a picture of a woman hanging from a rope.

"Mrs. River tied the rope to the rafter there," he points to a beam in the ceiling, "and jumped from the loft. From that height it was enough to snap her neck. This happened two weeks after Sandy was killed. The husband died in a construction accident six years before. The company was Treeman Oil and Gas."

He closes the file and walks out through the back door and around to the side of the house. Next to it are the three palm trees and an old oil jack pump slowly bowing up and down like a servant in front of a holy deity, in this case the deity is oil.

"This is the monster that killed little Sandy, she was only eight years old. Treeman Oil and Gas was responsible for maintaining the jack pumps. Two crewmen had arrived that day because the pump had stopped working the night before. Later, they reported it had been sabotaged. One of the men had gone back to the truck to return the tools, leaving the gate to the fence surrounding the pump open. The other was on the far side of the pump and could not see that the little girl had walked in. The pump was back in operation at that time."

May heard the repetitive sound as soon as she stepped out of the car. It was loud, painful even. Metal rubbing against metal, the screams of a child would be no match. To live beside this would drive any sane person mad.

"You have to understand that just about nothing stops these things. They are meant to run twenty four hours a day, three hundred and sixty-five days a year.

"Neither man heard a sound. It was Mathew that came out of the house looking for his sister and saw that she had been caught in the machinery, which was still going up and down, not caring that it had taken a young girl's life. The pictures are in the file and I don't want to see them ever again!

"At the time Mrs. River was working as a cook at the restaurant where we had lunch. It was a Saturday, no school. Mathew, only ten, was supposed to look after his sister. He and I were pretty good friends. We went to the same school and played on the same pee-wee baseball team. He was really smart but never had a break in life. He was born on the wrong side of the political dynasty. Here, if your blood line is that of the chief and council you live pretty well. We are fortunate, rich in oil and the casino revenue lets us live above the national average, but not so if you're from another clan.

"After the accident, he was put into the welfare system. It was downhill from that point on. The rest is all in the file." He stops for a moment. She thinks he is done, and she can tell it has exhausted him to tell this story again, probably for the umpteenth time. "We lost touch, but I did see him again. It was just after he had finished his training in the marines, and he was on leave before they sent him to Iraq. There was a disturbance call at the local newspaper. He had refused to leave and was accusing them of being complacent in the murder of his sister, covering up for Treeman. That was the last time I saw him."

May looks at her watch, if she leaves now, she can catch a flight and be back in Detroit tonight. "Thank you for the information and the file. One last question. Do you think he was involved in the Treeman kidnapping and the vandalism?"

"We followed up, but weren't able to connect him, like I said, he is smart. He had a lot of anger in him so..."

Chapter 73

He watched Linda Spalding enter her house on Chandler Park Drive. The house, a modest post World War II home was left to her by her father who passed away three years ago. She lived there alone with a cat for company.

He would go in late tonight and take her. Chloroform was his preferred method but he had the X26 Taser which could deliver up to 50,000 volts.

He watched her from his van, through her second-floor window. She was undressing with the curtains wide open. He imagined her posing after he had completed his masterpiece. Once she recovered both physically and mentally, she would accept her current situation. He would explain to her how he was going to make her a global star. He would hire the best photographer and promote her through all types of media. She would appear on billboards around the country, in magazines, newspapers and do interviews on the talk shows. He would show her the rest of the ransom money and offer it to her; the million dollars would be hers.

Chapter 74

May was able to get the last flight out. Unfortunately, the plane was full so she could not review the file that Detective Altaha had given her. She had updated Strouse on her findings. Now all the focus would be on apprehending Mathew River before he abducted his next victim. They had his physical description and a photograph as well as a sample of his DNA obtained from his service and prison records. She hoped his appearance had not changed dramatically. She tried to envision him with a shaved head, mustache or a full beard.

While waiting to board, she had caught up on her personal life. Calling both her parents, grandmother, Miles and Diane. Everyone seemed to be in a good mood, except for one. As soon as her mother had answered the phone, she knew by the sound of her voice that she was in trouble.

"You are getting married to a complete stranger and I had to hear it from your grandmother!" A stream of angry words came over the airwaves. "I have never even met the man, why are you keeping this from me? I talked to your father about it, and guess what, he already knew! Let me tell you, I won't be speaking to him for a long, long time."

"Mom, please calm down, his name is Robert Henderson. We have only met twice and that was just last week. We have a mutual interest and curiosity about the ring. He is an associate professor and is doing a paper on it. I think grandmother is having a little fun with you."

"Your grandmother told me you had gone out for dinner together and that you had invited him to lunch at her house. That sounds like a lot more than casual interest in a ring to me!"

Oh boy, grandma has gotten me into so much trouble. "When he called me, asking about the ring, we agreed to meet. I had no idea what he was like, so, like you always told me, meet him in a public place. That's it. As for the lunch at grandmother's, he wanted to know more about the ring's history, so I called her and asked if he could come over and see her collection of artifacts. She was the one who, unbeknownst to me, had arranged a pool side luncheon. This is mostly your mother's doing and she is goading you with it. Don't fall for it."

"That witch!"

"Mom, you know what she's like, she likes to play games."

"She is you know, she's a bonafied witch."

May knows her mother, and she feels bad. She should have told her. The best way forward was to give her some inside information. She puts a little excitement into her voice, like a schoolgirl telling secrets. "Now, full disclosure, he is very nice and I do like him. He's invited me to see Les Misérables on Saturday."

"A date! When do I get to meet him?"

Oh God. "Not necessarily a date, more like a reward for giving me some information that was helpful to the case I'm working on." Was that true or was she now lying to herself. Truth...she was excited to meet him again. "Mom, its way too early, lets see how it goes on Saturday. I promise to call you right afterwards and tell you all about it, ok?

"Well...all right, but you had better call."

"Love you mom, I got to go, they're boarding."

She listened to the jets taking off and landing and her mind begins to wander. Associate Professor Robert Henderson, why has he been on my mind?

"He is a good man, a serious man, not a man that would treat you like that Brandon character, use you for one night and discard you."

He is nice, isn't he, so thoughtful. *"He is a gentleman and treats you like you deserve to be treated. You know you like him. I know he would be a good father to your children."*

"Last call for boarding on flight 6531 to Dallas and Detroit, boarding from gate 24."

The announcement shocks her. What was that, it wasn't the usual conversation with herself, this was more like... someone was whispering in her ear, and that last phrase, '*I know he would be a good father to your children*' now that was something! She realizes that she has been twisting the ring around her finger.

She made one more call. It went to Dr. Salsburg voicemail, "Hi, it's May, can I get in to talk with you? I don't know what to do about my mother...and my love life."

Chapter 75

Styles is standing beside her old desk talking to a detective who is temporarily handling her missing person's cases while she is on assignment with the GAU. Strouse signals her to follow him, but they don't go to the conference room. Instead, he leads her to the fire escape staircase. A technician specialist from the forensic unit joins them.

"What is with the cloak and dagger stuff?" says Styles.

"George, tell her what you found."

"I was on the group that went through your apartment last night. Detective Strouse told me to look at your computer because Mathew River had voluntarily said he had accessed it. I looked at the browser history, checked to see if he copied any files etc. I noticed in the logs that someone had updated a file called *household expenses*."

"Yes, I do that for tax purposes." says Styles.

"Right, thing is, this update was done while you were in San Diego. I looked further and the file had been modified to link to a surveillance program. It would send an exact copy of every key stroke that was made on the computer to a server in India."

Strouse takes over the conversation, "Based on the level of sophistication and the risk he was willing to take by entering your home, I thought it might be prudent to check the GAU for similar spy ware. George did a thorough sweep of the conference room. He didn't find any tampering with the computer. But he did find a hidden microphone under my desk. We can't track where the receiver is, but it's new. It is reasonable to assume that Mr. River or one of his accomplices is behind this."

Strouse opens the door and says, "Thank you George."

Styles goes to follow but Strouse holds her back and closes the door.

"I hate to say this but considering what this character has done so far to infiltrate this investigation, I need to take extra precautions. You and I are going back into the conference room and giving him what he wants to hear. Let's keep this between us."

Styles stays quiet for a moment, "You think someone else may have been compromised!"

Strouse doesn't answer the question but says, "We left the mike in place, so everything has to sound normal. You ready?"

They return to the conference room and Strouse asks, "How was your trip?"

"Mostly a waste of time. The FBI and the locals claim they have nothing, which I think is bullshit. We are our own worst enemies.

I'm going to contact Homeland Security and see if they can act as an intermediary."

Strouse responds, "Worth a try, what do you have planned next?"

Her phone indicates that she has an incoming text message. She takes out her phone and looks at the screen. She shows it to Strouse and smiles. The message gives her the address where he has placed the one hundred thousand dollars, and she has one hour to retrieve it, or the deal is off the table.

"I need to take a few hours off to look for a new place for my dad. Then I'll update *the book*."

"Ok, take whatever time you need, family comes first."

Chapter 76

Strouse had set up a conference call with the team and told them that they would be taking the day off. They had been working nine days straight and would start again fresh on Thursday. He had suggested that they would review *the book* and see if they had missed some details because right now, they had reached a dead end.

He had hoped the conversation was being overheard and that he could lure River into thinking he could safely walk the streets. A BOLO had already been issued for a Mathew River to all police officers statewide. The police now had his picture and description and would be on the lookout for him. The squad would be interviewing known associates and former Midwest Joint Regional Correctional Facility inmates. Public CCTV cameras had been programmed to use facial recognition software in the search. Every bus, train station, airport, and traffic camera was scanning for his image. Over the last few years, DPD had asked major corporations for assistance in locating persons of interest. Many had given permission for the DPD to gain access to their security systems.

Strouse wasn't ready to ask for assistance from the media, believing that with the cash money he had, it would be too easy for him to go underground or flee the country.

Chapter 77

Styles used her own car to drive to the amusement park. There hadn't been enough time to set up electronic surveillance and the area was too open for undercover officers to blend in. They had analyzed the risk and stationed SWAT two blocks away in a plumbing truck.

Strouse felt there was little risk. River was trying to put Styles in a compromising position so that he would have leverage over her, not create conflict. He would be watching her take the money or more likely record the event. Unmarked police cars had been stationed at every major intersection around the area and a police helicopter was on standby.

Styles followed River's instructions to the letter. She arrived at the parking lot and drove around the van once to see if it was clear. Then she exited her vehicle. She found the key taped to the inside of the front left tire, just like the instructions said. She performed a thorough search but found nothing. No surveillance camera, no bomb and no money.

She jumped at the sound of her phone. It was River, the asshole was playing games.

"You will find the money in the sand box 50 yards from your current position on the corner of the parking lot." The call ended.

She went where she was told, found the bag and looked inside. There was a lot of money, nicely bundled into what appeared to be thousand dollar packets. Each packet containing 100 bills. She found nothing else in the bag.

Strouse had expected some type of tracker to be incorporated into the bag. He had told her to secure the bag at the train station in a locker. He didn't want it to be tracked back to the police station. Leaving it at her house was too risky. The transit authorities had been advised to arrest anyone that tried to gain access.

Chapter 78

May arrives at eight o'clock, carrying three cups of coffee and an assortment of donuts. Dr. Salsburg had brought in John Timmons, the hypnotist, to assist. She wanted May to be in a relaxed state with the hope of speaking to the alternate identity calling itself Adwoa Boateng again. She believed it was her that was causing May's anxiety disorder.

"Good morning, Dr. Salsburg, John. Sorry I couldn't make it yesterday but my connector flight out of Dallas got cancelled, mechanical problems. I wanted to apologize and hope this can show how much I care."

"Oh, those look fantastic," says John. "Here let me help you. Are these from Marybell's down the street? They are to die for."

Dr. Salsburg picks a chocolate eclair from the box and takes a bite, she smiles, enjoying its decadence.

They take a few moments to enjoy the coffee and treats. Then John begins. It takes less than ten minutes and May is fully under. He leaves the room while Dr. Salsburg has her session.

"May, would it be ok if I talked with Adwoa for a bit?"

"I don't know who that is Dr. Salsburg."

The voice changes, its stronger, one of someone in control, someone who has earned respect and demands the same.

"She has never known who I am or of my presents. It is a fundamental rule of the incantation. I am never allowed to tell her of my existence."

"Hello Adwoa, thank you for meeting me again."

"Well, it seems that you won't let this go, but if you are determined to mettle, perhaps you can be of some assistance."

Dr. Salsburg responds, "What is it that I can do for you Adwoa?"

"You claim to be a good friend to Mawusi. Is that true or is it all an act to get her to open up to you?"

"We have become very good friends. In fact I am considering ending our professional association because it could affect our relationship. Does it bother you that I'm her friend?"

"Perhaps not. In fact it is necessary for you to be a friend if you are going to be of assistance to us."

"And how is that? How can our friendship help you both?"

"For that, I will need to tell you a story, a story of how Mawusi and I became bonded. It happened many generations ago. A young girl, Massie was her name, she was my first. There have been many over the centuries, so many that I have forgotten some of their names.

"Massie loved to play by the river. One day a canoe came by with two men from a neighbouring tribe and abducted her taking her back to their village. She was raped by many of the men over

several days. Massie's father was a very powerful chief. He sent his warriors to kill all the men over the age of twelve. Twenty where slaughtered that day. Massie, as you would expect was traumatized to a point where she was going through life on autopilot, disconnected from her surroundings and her own feelings. You would now call it Post-Traumatic Stress Disorder (PTSD), you know, where the brain struggles to process overwhelming experiences. The chief ordered his healer, a shaman, to bring her back, and to make sure that his descendants would never be left to deal with something like this again. He loved his daughter very much.

"Barunde, the shaman, was unable to do so using traditional methods. She was afraid that the chief would banish her or even kill her. So, she reverted to using a spell. She summoned me. We struck a deal. I would rejuvenate Massie's spirit and protect her and in exchange I could live as long as Massie had female children through whom I could pass. She fashioned a ring to symbolize our agreement, a marriage between Massie and myself. If the female side ended, so would I. We agreed, but it was to be kept a secret. She was afraid of what the chief would do if he found out. This relationship could be described as ethereal and transformative. Massie became herself again and with my assistance, more aware of her surroundings. I gave her the ability to tell if people were dangerous, sharpened her reflexes, become intuitive towards people she met. It became a symbiotic relationship. I gave her guidance, protection, and sometimes power, while she serves as a vessel or companion. It became a sense of duality, as it bridges two realms—the physical and spiritual.

"She passed at the age of fifty five but gave birth to two girls, I chose the first to be my host.

"The agreement has been passed on to this day, sometimes the relationship was nurturing and enlightening, sometimes it was haunting and perilous. It has been beneficial to both, all the hosts have had long fruitful lives through this relationship. Do you now understand my dilemma...you should. You yourself had told a similar story to Mawusi the first meeting you had."

Malinda thinks back to the first meeting that they had. "We talked about the power I had that my siblings did not, which was that I could give my father grandchildren." She had told the story many times before, it was her favorite ice breaker.

"So, you are afraid that May, who is the only child will not have children and therefore your existence will end."

"I told you her name is Mawusi, it is her birthright, an honorable name meaning 'in the hands of God'! Yes, that would end my existence."

"And how do you see my involvement in helping you?"

"Mawusi has taken counter measures to prevent having children, this must be corrected."

"You are referring to a diaphragm or taking birth control pills."

"Yes, she has met a new man in her life, his name is Robert Henderson. She is growing attached to him. I think he would be a good match, and he wants to have children. She believes you are a good friend, one she can trust. You are in a position to advise her."

Malinda is shocked as to what Adwoa is proposing. She almost bursts out laughing at the thought. "Are you suggesting that I use my influence as her psychologist and friend, to encourage her to marry Robert Henderson and have his children?"

"Is it not your primary role as a therapist—and perhaps as a friend—to guide and counsel? You know as well as I do that nurturing and raising a child brings profound joy and purpose to life. I have existed for over four hundred years, and in each of my hosts, motherhood has been a source of renewal and connection. Do you truly believe that Mawusi—isolated as she is—would be the exception? She is lonely, adrift. A child could anchor her, give her a life filled with love and meaning. How can you deny her this possibility?"

"You're right, parenthood can bring a sense of fulfillment to many. But as her therapist, my role is not to impose what I believe would benefit her, but to empower Mawusi to make choices that reflect her own readiness and desires. This is her life, her body, her journey. While I recognize the potential joy and growth a child might bring, I must ask: Is this what she truly wants, or is it a yearning borne from your perspective and your need to continue your survival? It is my ethical obligation to respect her autonomy above all else. I will need to consider this conversation. This is something that I have never encountered before."

Malinda invites John back in to bring May out of hypnosis.

Chapter 79

Dr. Salsburg sits in her office and has poured herself a brandy. This is not what she had expected. Her first assessment of May was that she had a mild case of PTSD as a result of her involvement in the shooting. Then, it developed into Multiple Identity Disorder. Now, could it be something else...an entity, claiming to be over four hundred years old? She smiles. If she ever published a paper she would be laughed at. She had to laugh at herself for even thinking about it.

Then again, how crazy was the concept? Millions, even billions of people believed the holy spirit lived in them and had for over two thousand years. Even her own brother and sister fully embraced the idea. It happened with the sprinkling of water and the belief in a higher power. Wasn't that a spell?

Was this turning into a religious or a philosophical question? For certain, it was something above her pay grade. Perhaps she should consult a higher power herself. Make a call to her brother and ask him if he still truly believed that the Holy Spirit lived in him and if so, would it not be possible that other entities could also do the same?

She knew one thing, the well being of her client was the only concern...or was it? If, and only if the entity was real, did she have an obligation to it? If it was telling the truth, and if it had existed for over four hundred years and been a part of May/Mawusi for all her life, then wasn't she obligated to consider Adwoa as well?

Chapter 80

With a spring in her step, May walked the two blocks to her car. This was the second time that she had been hypnotized. The feeling for her was one of freedom, release, rest. She couldn't remember the sessions at all and didn't care. It was the results that counted and she liked it. There had been many instances when she was patrolling the streets when she encountered addicts in a daze from using cocaine or heroin, was this a similar rush?

She thought this would be a good time to call her mother. Her mother had felt left out and May had hurt her feelings by not telling her about Rob.

"Hey mom, how are you?"

"A sad voice responded "I'm ok, just doing laundry. Your dad is here, do you want to talk with him?"

"No, I thought that since it's your birthday next week I wondered if I could throw you a party, would you like that?"

A depressed voice came back "Oh, I don't need a party."

"I thought it would be nice, something small... I could invite Rob. I think you would like him."

"Well, maybe a party would be fun. Just a small one. Yes, do bring him."

"Ok, can we have it at your house, my apartment is too small for a party."

"Sure, I'll arrange the caterers and bartender. You bring the cake."

"Thanks mom, goodbye."

She could tell that this was all her mother needed.

Chapter 81

The DPD has twenty six hundred and thirty police officers spread over twelve precincts. Their headquarters is located in the Public Safety building where the highest number of officers are stationed. Fourteen percent of the officers are rated as detectives and almost half are located at headquarters.

None of the detectives report directly to Commander Ji-An, each of the departments has its own captain who has that responsibility. Most of her work is done on spreadsheets. However, six captains do report directly to her, and she feels that the relationship between the detectives, who number over one hundred and fifty in her building, and her captains, is indicative of how they are performing.

It is not her favorite thing to do, but every two to three weeks she leaves the comfort of her office to 'walk the floor' as she calls it. She'll spend half the morning hoping to catch most of them at their desks. Their names are all posted on the dividers, so she is confident in calling them by their last name. A few minutes will be spent with each one, asking them how their investigation is proceeding, what obstacles they may be encountering or just casual chit chat.

Detective Strouse is fortunate, he's in the conference room and spots her talking with one of the homicide detectives. It will be a few minutes before she gets to him. He removes the *Recording in Progress* sign that he has taped to the door and removes the bug from under his desk quietly placing both in the side drawer. He has told Captain Jackson about the device but is not sure if Captain Jackson has updated the chain of command.

Strouse picks up his coffee cup timing it so he will be exiting the conference room just as she approaches hoping to lure her away into a more public location. He doesn't want her buttonholing him into a long private conversation asking him awkward questions about the case or his team.

Unfortunately, she is up to his tricks and easily sidesteps him and plants herself in a chair. There is no one else in the room.

"Please sit down Detective, let's have a chat."

"Certainly Commander, I was just freshening up my coffee, can I get you a cup?"

"No thank you, I just had my tea. How is the GAU case coming along? I heard you made some major breakthroughs."

"We are very comfortable with our suspect in the case. His name is Mathew River. We have his picture distributed and are in the process of interviewing known associates."

"Good, let's hope he doesn't pick up another victim before we apprehend him. Any problems with the FBI?'

"So far, we've been able to keep them at arm's length. There's no proof that he's transported any of the victims over state lines, so they don't have jurisdiction at this point."

"And how is your team?" She looks around to see five empty desks. "All out in the field I see."

"I gave them the day off. They've all been working nine days straight."

"Captain Jackson told me that you added a new member to your team, Detective Judy Styles, how is she working out?"

Shit, this is what he wanted to avoid. He has no idea how much Jackson has told the Commander regarding the attempt to bribe her into spying on the GAU.

He tries to sidestep the question with misdirection. "Yes, she worked closely with Detective May Sheppard before in Missing Persons. We thought she would be a good fit."

"I see, and how is our rookie Ms. Sheppard doing?"

This is the second time she has asked him about her performance. What is so special about this girl that a two star would be asking about her? Is this her end game, is this what this conversation is all about, May Sheppard?

Ji-An reads his thoughts, "I'm just asking because I feel somewhat responsible for her. I see great potential in her, but I wonder if my recommending her for the GAU team may have been premature considering her lack of experience as a detective."

"She has performed above my expectations and is definitely a key asset. Really enthusiastic with fantastic instincts, she leaves the rest of the team behind at times."

"I'm pleased you recognize her tendency to march off on her own. I understand it happened again at the reservation in New Mexico. Fortunately, it turned out well. I'm confident that you are the right person to help guide her in these situations and that you feel as responsible as I do for her wellbeing and development. Thank you for your time, Detective Strouse. According to Captain Jackson, he thinks you have good leadership skills." She stands and continues her tour.

Strouse sits back in his chair wondering how Ji-An had known about the trip to the reservation and that May had gone there on her own. He considered calling Ji-An's personal assistant to get some inside information. They had had a short affair two years ago which ended with them both going to neutral corners. They still liked each other, just not in the same bed. She was very loyal to her boss, and he figured she would not be very forthcoming. He would use that card when he needed it for his own self-preservation. Ji-An had given him a clear warning. Keep her on a very, very short leash, and he would do just that.

Chapter 82

He had done his research. People typically experience their deepest sleep during the first half of the night, particularly in the first two sleep cycles. Deep sleep, also known as slow-wave sleep (SWS), occurs in stage 3 of non-rapid eye movement (REM) sleep, and it plays a crucial role in physical restoration, memory consolidation, and immune function.

Each sleep cycle lasts about 90–110 minutes, and deep sleep is most prominent in the early part of the night before REM sleep becomes more dominant in later cycles.

The bedroom light went out at eleven PM. He waited in the van until just past one thirty. He picked up the satchel containing his tools and exited the vehicle. She had installed a doorbell camera, so he simply used the back entrance. He put on his mask and gloves and lifted his hoodie. A small pry bar was all he needed to open the door. He turned on the light mounted on his forehead and took out the zip lock bag containing the piece of cheese cloth that was already moistened with chloroform. Her bedroom was upstairs. It was an old house, and he was surprised that the steps did not creak under his one hundred and eighty pound weight. It helped that it had been carpeted. There were only two rooms upstairs, both were bedrooms. There was one bathroom, and it was on the main floor just across from the stairs. She would be in the bedroom to the right based on the light he saw coming from the window earlier. The door was open and he could see her reflection in the dresser's mirror. She was laying on the left side of a queen size bed and was wearing a white night shirt. One shoulder was bare. He admired her for a moment. She would be the perfect model. The sheet and blanket had been pushed to the side. It had been warm for the past week, and the house did not have air conditioning.

He had learned from experience that most women will use their fingernails to defend themselves. So, he took the precaution of pulling the blanket up to her neck making sure that her arms and hands would be restricted. He removed the chloroformed cloth from the bag and laid it softly over her mouth and nose until she began to struggle. He then applied pressure and dropped his full weight on her body. It took only twenty seconds before she stopped moving. He placed duct tape over her mouth and used zip ties to restrain her wrists behind her back and around her ankles.

He returned to the van and drove it down the back lane, parking it next to the small garage. From the back of the van he removed the oversized suitcase that had four wheels. She would easily fit into it. As he rolled it down the stairs the thought occurred to him that the DNA from every one of the girls he had abducted could probably be found in the case. He considered himself to be in good physical shape, the marines had seen to that. Half an hour later he was back on the highway and forty minutes from his rented farmhouse.

Chapter 83

Diane is already sitting on the patio. It's a beautiful afternoon and she has arranged to meet at the Roostertail, a historic waterfront venue with beautiful views of the Detroit River. It was a great spot for a relaxing meal with a picturesque backdrop. She gets up to greet May and gives her a hug with a peck on both cheeks. May is a little surprised, it's not Diane's usual greeting. A waiter is standing by to assist with the seating, but just as he does, Malinda comes through the door and the greeting is repeated.

"Malinda speaks first, "Well what is this great news that you want to tell us about?"

Diane responds by holding up her trigger finger and waves it in the air. "Not so fast ladies. We need some cocktails first.

"Derrick dear, will you please bring these two ladies their beverage of choice." May asks for a Kokanee and Malinda requests a Pino Grigio. Before the waiter can turn to fill the order Diane points to her Martini glass and says, "I'll have another one of these."

May looks at Malinda, and says to Diane, "Been here awhile, have you?"

"I wanted to get a good table before the lunch hour rush. To change the subject, how is your new lover performing?"

May looks at Diane with an open mouth, expressive eyes and a sense of shock. "We've only known each other for a week, and if he was my lover during that time, and I'm not saying he was, he would no doubt have performed like a star."

Malinda gets into the action by saying, "Rumor has it that as lovers go, Brandon set the bar."

May lifts her chin, turns her head and says, "Oh look, here come the drinks."

May takes her glass of beer and drinks from it. "That is soooo good," and smiles.

"Would you like to place your orders ladies?"

Diane speaks first, "Well to stimulate the current topic of conversation, we should order a large plate of oysters as a starter, don't you think girls?" They all break out in laughter.

It's clear that the waiter has missed a private joke and goes off to fill the order. He returned shortly and they all indulged, stopping only briefly to continue their laughter.

"Ok, we're dying to know. Why did you invite us here on such short notice?"

Diane pauses for a brief moment and says, "Miles had invited me for dinner yesterday. He had booked a table at the Monarch Club." She opens up her purse and the girls think she is retrieving lip gloss or a tissue, but instead she opens a small box and under the table slides on a ring.

"He starts by telling me that he's going to leave the force. He says the hip is not letting him give one hundred percent to the job, and he doesn't want to sit behind a desk. I feel for him, he loves his life as a police officer. He then tells me that he's been offered a job to head the loss prevention unit at Stellantis North America as a security adviser."

Malinda speaks up, "That was formerly Chrysler, right?"

"Yes, so I thought last night was a promotional celebration, but instead he gets off his chair and drops to one knee and pulls this out." She lifts her hand from under the table and waves it at the girls.

May jumps up and grabs her wrist. "Oh My God. Look at it. He swore to me that he wouldn't marry anyone other than me, and I believed him. You Bitch." She waves over the waiter, "Derrick, can you get us a bottle of champagne please, we're going to celebrate."

Malinda takes a good look at the ring, it was beautiful. A nice size pink rock, surrounded by emeralds. Green is Diane's favorite color. "When is the wedding?"

"Here is the problem. I insisted that we get married right away because there's no chance I'm letting him get away. She takes a deep breath, "So, I am going to need a lot of help. This is going to happen in three weeks, will you two be my maids of honor? I know you both have careers that keep you busy, but I can't, I don't want to do this by myself. I really need your help."

May and Malinda face each other, raise their hand and do a high five. "We are going to have so much fun, thank you for letting us share this with you."

"Let's start planning, how many guests will be invited? Let's go pick out the dresses."

Chapter 84

He had her mildly sedated and undressed. He had applied the sensors to remotely monitor her vitals. Sedating someone for a long period had risks. She should sleep comfortably throughout the night. He covered her with a blanket and put a pillow under her head. It was now four thirty in the morning and he was tired. He looked around the basement, it had taken a lot of work to get it into the condition that it was. He had framed a ten by ten room with two by six studs, covered the ceiling and walls with soundproofing materials, then added two sheets of half inch drywall. The farmhouse was situated in a remote location, not visible from the road or from his neighbors. Even if someone else entered the house it was unlikely she would hear them or them her. He installed electrical and ventilation. He chose an exterior door because it was insulated and was metal clad. For security he had added a dead bolt and cameras.

When he was in her house he had spotted her music collection. It was not the type of music he listened to when he worked but thought it would help calm her, so he downloaded songs by the same artists.

He had realized that the relationship between her and the others would need to be different. He had thought of them as canvasses, they were not people. Now, he needed to have a partner. Someone who was willing to carry his message. To expect her friendship would be unrealistic, the best he could hope for was to convince her that this could be a mutually beneficial relationship. She would be famous and wealthy. He would get his revenge.

He had called Detective Styles while waiting for Linda Spalding to retire for the night. She had told him that the team had a lead on a person of interest and was following up. His name was Kalev Hissan. He had been a student at the College of Fine, Performing and Communication Arts. He had been dismissed from the school when he had assaulted one of the models.

It sounded like a plausible theory because it ran parallel to his own story.

Chapter 85

Detective Holland and May had been assigned to interview a cellmate at Marine Corps Brig, Camp Pendleton in California. Mathew's service record showed that he had served time there. They set up a video conference call with a Jesus Martinez who had the lower bunk. After examining his record, it was discovered that they had become close friends but just before Mathew was released, there was a falling out.

Jesus was more than willing to shed disparaging information on his cellmate and about his plans after being released. Jesus himself would be serving another three years for aggravated assault on an officer.

It turned out that Mathew had applied to several higher educational art institutions while at Pendleton. His application had been rejected by many but if nothing else, Mathew was persistent. He continued to adjust his submission, making changes where needed. He finally received a letter from the College for Creative Studies in Detroit accepting him into the program the following year.

Jesus had received one letter from Mathew after his release. It was short but expressed how he had outsmarted the college and was enjoying higher education while he, Jesus, was peeling potatoes in prison.

They went to the College for Creative Studies and spoke to the associate professor. She remembered Mathew who had attended her classes for three months. She believed he had raw talent but without the background training required to proceed at the class level that his application indicated, he would not be able to advance. She suggested that he start as a first year student. He dismissed her suggestions and never returned.

The next step was to go to the administration building and speak with the registrar in the hopes of obtaining a place of residence for one Mathew River. They gave his address without issue. Forty minutes later they were at his building talking to the landlord. He also remembered Mathew even though he had stayed there for only four months and the lease had been for one year. He had paid the additional eight months in cash as he had the previous four months. No, he did not leave a forwarding address.

May asks, "Do you know if he had any friends that we could talk to? A neighbor perhaps, who could give us an idea as to where to find him?"

"Your best chance is to go down to the end of the block. You will see Petron's, it's a Mexican American restaurant. He would go there almost every night for dinner."

It was lunch time and Mexican sounded as good as any other place, so they walked to the corner.

It was small, only five tables. It looked like it had been there for forty years.

"What are you going to have?" asks Holland. "Do you want to share a plate of Nachos?"

May looks up at him. He is three inches taller than her and weighs in at two hundred and ninety pounds. Most of it is muscle. He doesn't want people to look at him like he is a big ape, so his suits are a size too big on him. It doesn't work, it only makes him look more menacing. A voice tells her that she will not get an equal share. "I'm in the mood for fajitas." She sees the disappointment in his face.

The waitress is twenty years her senior. "Good afternoon, folks, I haven't seen you here before. Welcome to Petron's, my name is Carmen. How can I help you?"

They place their orders. Holland asks for a double order of hot wings, May orders fajitas.

The food turns out to be better than good. When Carmen returns with the bill May gives her a credit card and adds a twenty dollar bill as a tip. The waitress takes note.

May opens her phone and shows her a picture of Mathew River. "Do you know this man? We've been told that he used to frequent here a year or two ago?"

"Oh, sure that's Mathew. We don't get too many Apache here, so you tend to remember. He still comes in occasionally but not like before. He used to come in every night except for Mondays when we are closed."

"How often does he come by?"

"Usually once a week, the day varies. He seems like a nice boy always polite and a good tipper."

May looks at Holland. She considers asking the waitress to give her a call the next time he comes in, but something deep inside her tells her to take another approach.

Holland gets up and thanks the waitress. They exit the restaurant.

Holland speaks , "She likes him, I don't think she's going to give him up."

"I think you're right. Best we stake out the place and wait for him to show. If he comes in on a weekly basis, it shouldn't take long."

"Let's call Strouse, see if he'll set up a schedule for the stakeout. We can park down the street and keep an eye on the place until he gets us relief." says Holland.

Chapter 86

"It's been two hours, what's taking them so long?" Holland is in the driver's seat and he's starting to fidget.

"I'll give her a call, see what's keeping them". May takes out her phone and taps Styles' name. "Hey, the natives are getting restless, what's your ETA? There is a pause and May says "thirty minutes?"

"Ok."

She looks at Holland, "If you need to go to the bathroom, there's a garage two blocks north. I can wait here."

"You heard what Strouse said at the meeting this morning as well as I did, in fact I'm pretty sure he was looking at us when he said it. We stick together as a team until this is finished, and besides, I don't need to go to the bathroom, I'm thirsty."

"That's what you get for ordering two servings of hot wings." She looks at him and decides to add a little fuel to his fire. "Pretty sure I saw a drink machine next to the door. Said ice cold water and soft drinks on it. You could be there in two minutes, grab yourself a cold one and be back before anyone is the wiser."

She sees him lick his lips. This is fun. "Or perhaps they sell those strawberry shakes inside, I would go for one of those, call it my treat."

He continues to look straight ahead with his left eye on the front door of the restaurant but swings his right eye to look at her. Creepy is the word that comes to her mind. Like in Chucky the movie.

"Cut that out, it gives me the willies when you do that."

"We'll stick to the plan, each team will do a two hour shift. If we spot him, we bring in the rest of the team while he's eating. Then all of us follow him back to his hidey hole. Strouse is concerned that he may already have his next victim drugged and restrained there. If we take him here, he may use that information as a bargaining chip or just let her die on his table. It's a good plan and I am not going to be the one to screw it up. Strouse is maybe five foot eight but you don't want to piss him off. I have seen that and prefer to stay on his good side."

A fly had gotten into the car and is buzzing around. With the blistering speed of a mongoose, he snaps it out of the air with his right thumb and forefinger. Holland squeezes it to death. So much for the rumor that the big guy couldn't hurt a fly.

Chapter 87

Mathew sits on the porch, with his evening coffee. He has his Samsung tablet next to him so that he can monitor her vitals and see if she has awakened. He needs to rethink his whole approach. He can't believe how stupid he's been, thinking that his previous choices would have co-operated with him. What in the world would they benefit from such an arrangement?

This time it would be more mutually advantageous. He had already made some changes. The room had been transformed from a sterile look to one more like a hotel. He would sit with Linda and explain his goals and why he needed to achieve them. He would show how this could benefit her. He didn't need her collaboration, the tattooing was going to happen, but if she cooperated it could be positive.

He had used fear as a weapon with the other girls. That had worked for a while but based on the news articles, it hadn't taken hold for as long as he had hoped. Two of them had given a brief description of their abduction.

His reasoning had been all wrong there as well. He naturally assumed that because the girls had dedicated their study to the arts, they too would see beauty in his work, and it had been beautiful. Thousands of people paid hard earned money to be tattooed. There were magazines and TV shows on the subject. Over time they should have accepted the situation and embraced his work. Instead, they showed anger and hostility in the article.

Fear had not worked, and it would not be used on Linda Spalding. He had brought in an old laptop computer and loaded the video that he had taken when he tattooed the other girls. He had also scanned articles from the newspapers that had stated the girls had been released without being harmed. He had left out the parts that said they had been hospitalized and at least one had been treated for PTSD. He had hoped Linda would view them and see that the girls had not been harmed and therefore give her hope that she wouldn't be harmed either. The computer didn't have an internet connection and was used to test applications.

The other girls (he now accepted that they were more than just a canvas) had been secured with Velcro straps. Linda would be allowed to move around the room.

A more comfortable environment, freedom of movement, music, an open relationship, it was a good start, but he knew there was more to do to win her over. For now, though, he too needed sleep. Tomorrow morning, he will go and pick up some more supplies and have breakfast at his favorite restaurant.

Chapter 88

Styles stands at the doorway to the conference room and says to Strouse, "Going for a coffee, do you want one?"

"I could use a break, I'll join you."

In the stairway she gives him the news. "Just checked the missing persons list. I think we have another one. The only difference is that she isn't in the art world precisely. She is a model."

"How long has she been missing?"

"She was last seen by her agent yesterday at eight PM. He's the one who reported her missing, she was to be at a photo shoot this morning at nine. We've been making exceptions on the reporting time required for anyone that looks like our victims."

Strouse takes out his phone and calls Holland. "Anything happening?"

"All's quiet."

"There is a fifty-fifty chance he has his next victim. It's absolutely critical that he doesn't spot you. Is there a building that you can see the restaurant from and take up a position there?"

Holland looks around, "There's a four story apartment building across the street, some of the units may be empty. We could knock on a door and see if they'll help us out. If we're lucky the landlord may let us in."

"Do that, then move the tail car back another two blocks. I'll send Styles there with a tracker. When you spot River see what car he's driving. If it's out of his view when he's in the restaurant you two will go down and install it. We can't risk him detecting that we are onto him. If it's not safe to install the tracker we'll go with the original plan." He doesn't wait for a response and disconnects the call.

He turns to Styles, "Let's go back to the conference room and you can tell me about the missing girl and hope he's listening. We need to shake him up, maybe he'll make a mistake. If he calls you, tell him that she's missing and the precinct is going nuts trying to find her. Then take the tracker and deliver it to Holland and Sheppard. Don't drive anywhere near the restaurant. I'll arrange for a helicopter to be on standby and we'll track him that way."

Holland had been able to find a vacant apartment on the third floor with a good view of the restaurant and the street below. May had called Strouse back and suggested that they bring in some cars from the impound center and park them in front of the restaurant so that Mathew wouldn't find a spot. This would make it difficult for him to observe his car while he was having his meal. This would decrease the likelihood that they would be spotted when installing the tracker.

Styles arrived, but Mathew didn't. They all went home when the restaurant closed at eight that night. They would be back before it opened the next morning.

Chapter 89

Linda Spalding wakes up to a massive headache, naked and confused. She looks around the room. There is a large overhead light like you would see in an operating room, but it's not turned on. The room is softly lit by three pole lamps. She is laying on what looks like a hospital bed. Immediately she imagines herself in a horror movie. She is afraid to remove the covers. What has he done, is my kidney missing? She doesn't feel pain except the screaming headache. Slowly she lifts the sheet and blanket. Everything is in place, no bandages are visible. She feels her face and head. She still has her hair.

She continues to survey her surroundings. There's a chair in front of a small office desk. On it is a laptop computer. Next to the desk is a comfortable reading chair and end table which has a large plastic pitcher of water and matching glass. Next to it is a bottle of Advil. Her mouth is parched. Removing the sensors, she sits up and steps from the bed to pour herself some water. She removes the cap from the Advil and finds that it still has the factory seal on it. She drinks half the water and opens the bottle. Takes out three pills, then changes her mind and adds one more. While she drinks, she continues to look around and spots two doors. She knows they are going to be locked but checks them just the same. The first one leads to a small bathroom. She opens every drawer in the vanity, nothing but soap, some feminine hygiene products and toilet paper. The second door is locked. She hammers at it and starts to scream, but the pain in her head stops her. At the end of the bed there is a bundle of clothing. Sweatshirt and pants, a pair of wool slippers. The room is cool, so she puts them on. In each corner, next to the ceiling, are cameras. She doesn't see anything she could use as a weapon to defend herself or tool to pry open the door.

Finally, she sits in front of the computer and turns it on. There is a power cord but no ethernet cable. Perhaps it has WIFI, and she can get a message out to...DPD, her agent, the list is short. She hits the power button. The Windows Ten logo appears. The time and date in the bottom right hand corner tells her she has been here for six hours. There's no request for a password. The home screen shows only a folder with several files in them, a Word file named Manifesto.docx, Master plan.docx, Contact.csv, Interviews.mp4 and Maps.gpx. As expected, the system setting shows that there is no router within range.

She uses the pointer to click on a file called 'Interview'. The face of an American Indian comes into focus. "Good morning, Linda...

Chapter 90

At eight-fifteen a white panel van drives slowly and turns the corner disappearing out of sight from Holland. Traffic is heavy this time of day as there is a large high school down the street. A steady stream of cars has been going past the restaurant for the last half hour. Holland spots a man that could be Mathew, so he picks up the binoculars to have a closer look. Yes, definitely him.

"He's here."

May grabs the camera and takes several pictures. "Did you see which vehicle he was driving?"

Holland lowers the binoculars and watches as Mathew walks into the restaurant. "It could be any one of the last three vehicles that turned the corner, or he could have come from the other direction."

Holland picks up his phone. "Ok, I'm going to call it in, see what the boss wants us to do."

Strouse is in his car when his phone rings. He activates his hands free unit. "What you got?"

"He just walked into the restaurant by himself. Positive ID, but we don't know which vehicle he was in. He came around from a blind corner."

"Alright, have May go down and look around for a likely vehicle and attach the tracker if possible. If she can, find a spot where she can observe the area that he most likely came from, have her stay there. You keep an eye out from your location. I'll send the other two teams to cover the other corners. I'm on my way as well, give me fifteen minutes."

May was within earshot of the conversation and grabbed the tracker and is on her way out before he even ends the call. As she turns the corner from the direction that Mathew came from, she finds the street is long with several retail and specialty stores. There are plenty of parking spaces available. She walks down the street to the first car, it's a small Toyota. She thinks about what type of vehicle a kidnapper would use for successfully abducting multiple girls. There are two vehicles that would meet her criteria further down the street. A dark blue half ton with a cab over the back and the white panel van Holland saw turn the corner. As she walks towards them, she passes a small hardware store, a pizza parlor, a drug store, a nail salon and a medical supply store. She chooses the van, and has a good look around to see if anyone is watching. The van is parked in front of a video arcade store with large plate glass windows. It's packed with teenagers and there's no way that she could attach the tracker without being spotted. She moves to the truck which is parked four spots further down. There is still heavy traffic but not too many people in a position to spot her.

She takes the tracker from her pocket, kneels down and attaches it to the frame of the truck. She pulls on it to make sure that the magnet will hold fast.

She continues walking down the sidewalk discreetly taking pictures with her phone of every car that she passes making sure that she also gets the plate number, and circles the block. She types a message to the team on her phone identifying the truck as the one she had put the tracker on. Back at the apartment she finds that Strouse has already arrived and tells him the story about the van. He takes out the phone and calls dispatch to request the chopper.

"Ok, here's the plan. The chopper will follow the truck, the team will stake out the block from every side and hope we can see which vehicle he gets into. If it's the truck, we let the chopper take it from there. If it's another vehicle we follow it. We have three units. A half ton with Ontario plates, which will be manned by team one. The minivan with Mark's Carpet Cleaner logo on the side will be team two, and the sedan with the baby seat at the back will be for you two. We will do the hopscotch thing. Team one, then team two and so forth. Never stay on him for more than one turn."

Fifteen minutes later Mathew makes his exit and walks around the corner and gets into the van. Holland is there and calls it in. Strouse gets on the phone and cancels the helicopter. He tells May to retrieve the tracker from the truck while Holland goes and gets the sedan. They should be able to catch up if they hustle. Everything goes as planned and they switch lead cars three times. They have been steadily moving and are almost out of the suburbs. Traffic is heavy but manageable on this three lane road until they reach a construction site forcing everyone into a single lane. Team two has the lead and is three cars behind Mathew but one lane over. Mathew's van passes through the construction zone and the lead car is now ten cars back after merging into the single lane. A flag man suddenly steps into traffic to give the right of way to a dump truck. It takes two long minutes for traffic to flow again. The van was not spotted again even though the teams toured the area for an additional ten mile radius.

Chapter 91

Linda is getting tired, she has viewed the videos and read all the documents. It has taken her almost four hours. Her stomach is starting to rumble but the headache is gone. She thinks over his plan. The idea of using tattoos as a gateway to entice the media into taking interest in his story was certainly unique. The planning and investment he has made undoubtedly proves his determination.

Based on what she has read and seen, his life has been a tragedy. The death of his little sister, for which he blames the oil company, his tribe and lastly himself. The suicide of his mother. Being mistreated in almost every foster home of which there were ten. His time spent in prison, which he admits was his own fault, tells a story of someone that was dealt a bad hand. She realizes that she's feeling sorry for him.

She muses if it could work, presuming that he had three things go right. First, he would need a willing subject to be the messenger. Second, he would need time to complete the work. It sounds like he has already hired an advertising agency to manage the project, scheduled the magazine advertisements, and billboards. These have already been invoiced and paid for.

He has scanned in the receipts for each one. The last thing he needed was to have the photos of his work taken. She has heard of Brett Rounders and seen some of his work. He definitely knows how to make a woman look good.

She moves to the large chair, crosses her legs and drinks the last of the water.

Her career has been stagnating. She is behind on her property tax and is concerned that unless things pick up, she may lose the house. Her father's house. The one he worked so hard to buy and maintain. The one he left for her. The question was, would things pick up? Her agent had made subtle suggestions about taking classes in accounting because she was good with numbers. The number 28 kept coming up. It also happened to be her age. How long did she have left before the body didn't look as striking as it used to?

She goes back to the computer and opens the file with his drawings. They tell the story of his sister's death at the hands of Treeman Oil and Gas. Considering the subject matter, she finds them fascinating, beautiful even. The colors are brilliant. He has created several consecutive sketches as inspiration for Brett Rounders to draw on. There are three she especially likes of a woman wearing only native jewelry sitting by a glowing fire. Several others were wearing only a chief's head-dress made of eagle feathers. And her favorite is of a woman, naked, sitting on a horse holding a spear like Lady Godiva. They look really beautiful. It was true art. The tattoos covered most of the body from front to back and from shoulders to the mid-thigh. She had never seen colors like that on a tattoo. She herself has never had a tattoo, but there have been times... Some of her associates have had multiple tattoos, most look really good on them. She had asked, what was it like, did it hurt? The stories varied with the person, but in the end, they all claimed it was worth the discomfort and the cost.

She wondered what they would look like on her. He had photographs of the girls whom he had partially tattooed and placed them in the file. She had heard about them on the news, but she had never seen them. They had been released. There was no mention of sexual assault, had it happened to her while she was unconscious? There was no indication that it had. She had also seen articles and a news video about a twelve year old girl in California who had been abducted and that a ransom of over a million dollars had been paid for her release. She too had been set free unharmed.

Her fear had diminished after reading the articles. It seemed to indicate he was not out to hurt anyone.

His offer to make her famous and paying her a million dollars begins to open so many possibilities.

Chapter 92

May comes through the door and is disappointed that John is not there. "Is John running late?"

Dr. Salsburg stands up and greets May with a hug and a kiss on the cheek. "Come and sit down, John won't be joining us anymore at my request. I think hypnotherapy has had its benefits but has reached its limit.

"I want to meet with you today to talk about what I have discovered and where we/you go from here. These sessions have revealed to me that the shooting death in which you were involved has affected you more than you'll admit. It has manifested a deeply suppressed belief instilled in you by your grandmother when you were young.

"There are many influences in our daily lives that on the surface can appear benign but sometimes, they can reveal themselves in surprising ways, especially after a traumatic experience. This stimuli can be from social media, peer pressures, religious influences, traditional customs, the list goes on. Most of the time we don't notice the impact of these encounters, but sometimes they express themselves in more fundamental ways. When that happens, we may not even know it. Take fight or flight as an example. In most situations, you don't have time to think about it. You do it. What made you choose one over the other?

"In your case, the shooting has brought out an alternate personality solely focused on protecting your survival and that of your blood line. The tales of your grandmother and her past in Africa, the pressures placed upon you to produce an heir from your parents, and your own self survival instincts has started to influence your decisions without you knowing it. These can all be of great value to you. They have already sharpened your skills as a detective. Just keep them in mind as you move forward. You are your own person, make your own choices.

"Now, I have gone as far as I can, or more honestly, as far as I want to. You have become my closest friend. In good professional conduct I can no longer be your psychologist, so this will be our last session. If you wish to continue therapy, I can recommend someone."

May is shocked by this news. She sits for a moment taking in what she has just been told. Finally, she gets up, crosses the divide and hugs her best friend and former therapist. Tears roll down both their cheeks.

Chapter 93

"Sorry that I was so long, traffic was heavy due to construction."

The sound coming from the computer startles Linda, she realizes that she has dozed off. She moves to the computer and sees Mathew on the screen. "Have you had a chance to consider my offer?"

How is this happening, there is no internet connection? Maybe there is a cellular link. "I have, under three conditions!"

"Ok, list away."

"One, I want to see the money, not a cheque, the real money, in cash, right here where I can inspect it."

"Done. I have it right here in a duffel bag. It's yours to walk out the door with, right after the pictures are taken. The whole thing can be over within three to four days. It's partly up to you, how much discomfort you can handle. I can give you a sedative or put you out completely if you want to speed up the process."

"Secondly, what's your plan after I'm released? You know the police will be looking for me. You've already admitted in these videos that you have kidnapped at least seven people and held them against their will."

"As soon as this is done, I will surrender myself to the police. I have been monitoring their progress, and they know who I am. It will only be a matter of time before they find me. If I surrender with the aid of a lawyer, there is less chance that I'll be killed during a man hunt. I want to tell my story in court, I can't do that if I'm dead.

"What we need to think about is your story."

Linda is confused. "My story?"

"Yes, when they arrest me, I'm going to tell them everything that happened, as far back as I can remember. How my family was treated by the band. How we were treated by the Treeman Oil and Gas Company and how my mother and I were treated and discarded by the justice system and the press. I will tell them that I abducted Treeman's daughter. That I abducted six, no seven women here in Detroit and tattooed them against their will. But I won't tell them about our bargain. I won't tell them that you took the rest of the money. I'll say that I spent most of it and that the rest was lost at the racetrack. I have gone there a few times so there will be video of me if they want to check. That's the story I'll tell. I won't say that you co-operated in any way. You were abducted, just like the others. What story will you tell? How will you explain your sudden wealth?"

She thinks about what he has said, it makes sense. "You're right, I'll need to think about that." She considers this for a moment but can't come up with an answer.

"The third thing. I want a proper breakfast, I'm starved."

"That will take a little longer than bringing the money down to you. How does twenty minutes sound, eggs, bacon, tacos and beans? Coffee?"

"Bring the coffee with the money first."

Chapter 94

It has been five days since they last saw Mathew River, and no one has reported any sign of him. They checked out the license plate that was on the van, but it had been stolen from a similar van that had been sitting in a scrap yard for months. They went back to the restaurant and interviewed everyone that worked there and asked if he ever talked about where he lived, what he did, who he knew. Did he ever pay by credit card? Did they see him drive a different car? Did he ever dine with anyone else?

The GAU researched every aspect of Linda Spalding's history hoping to see when he came into her life. They found a security video at a residence two doors from her home that showed a white van parked near her house late at night. It recorded a man wearing a hoodie get out and move toward her residence. About forty minutes later he returned to the van and drove off. It didn't prove that he took her, but everyone accepted that they had failed to stop another abduction. They continued to watch the restaurant.

No one had any new ideas or leads to follow. The team was sitting back, hoping that a new lead would miraculously present itself.

May became frustrated as did the rest of the team. She pulled out a city map and used a highlighter to trace the route they had taken when they had followed the van. Maybe he had spotted them and drove right past his hideout so that he could shake them and then take a roundabout way back. She then plotted the route on Google Earth to get a bird's eye view of each building. Nothing of note was discovered. She drove the same route every day at different times hoping to spot the van.

On the fifth day she taps Holland on the shoulder. "Come on, I want to do the whole thing again but start right where his van was parked."

"Better than sitting here."

It was eight thirty, just about the same time that River left the restaurant. They were parked in the same spot that he had parked in. The street was almost empty of parked cars, but there was heavy road traffic, just like it was that day.

May is sitting behind the wheel. "Ok, we'll take the exact same route but take it slow and have a good look around." She starts the car and pulls out, traveling twenty miles per hour. She gets to the corner and stops. '*Go back, you have gone too far, start over and take the blinders off.*' She steps on the gas and makes a left turn.

Holland gives her a look, "This is not the way he went, he went straight, I'm positive."

"I just thought of something, work with me." She circles the block and parks in the same spot as before and puts the car in park, kills the engine.

"What's going through your head?"

She takes a moment "Why does he drive all the way here so often, is it just the food?"

Holland cocks his head, "It's pretty good but not great."

"Well, why did he park so far from the restaurant? There were plenty of empty parking spots available once you turn the corner. He parked more than halfway down the street and walked all the way back. Doesn't that seem strange to you?"

Holland gets out of the car, "Let's take a walk down the street, see what we see."

They are both standing beside the car and looked up at a sign on the building in front of them. *Thompson Brothers – Medical Supply Company*. The building next door was *Detroit Veterinary Supplies*. The following building is the arcade.

"Looks like one stop shopping for someone setting up their own clinic" says May, "and I'm in a shopping mood."

Holland leads the way and opens the door to Thompson Brothers to let May in. "Always a gentleman." she says.

There is a young girl at the counter and she gives them a kind smile, "Can I help you folks?" They both take out their badges and May pulls out a five by seven photo of Mathew River. "Have you ever seen this man. He might have been here five days ago, or possibly several times in the last year."

She looks at the photo, "No, but I only work here part time and am usually in the back. I can call Tim, he usually works the front counter."

"Thank you, that would be great."

She calls Tim, a man about forty years old and Holland asks him the same question. "Yes, he comes in here quite often. I would say that he's been here a few times this year already."

May asks, "When was the last time?"

"That was just on Tuesday morning around eight, we had just opened. He bought a new mattress, some sheets and a pillow. I helped him load them into the van."

May asks "How did he pay, was it with a credit card? Does he have an account with you?"

"What is this all about?"

Holland speaks up with an angry tone in his voice, "Just answer the detective's question!"

"Ok, he always pays with cash and if you are looking for an address, we did deliver some of the bigger stuff to his place about eight months ago."

May in her sweetest voice, "and would you still have that address and phone number?"

Tim gives Holland a nervous look, "I think I can find that in the back."

Holland comes around the counter and follows him to the back.

When they leave the store May says, "Did you have fun scaring the shit out of poor Tim?"

Holland just gives her a smile and points to the Veterinary store next door "Had a blast. Let's do it again but this time you can be the Godzilla."

"I don't think so, let's stick to the script." They went in and talked with the manager. Shortly after leaving the store, May punches in the address on her phone Map app. "Do you want to do a drive-by and see what the place looks like before going back to the GAU and updating Strouse?"

"Can't see any harm in just driving by and seeing what the area looks like, maybe check in with some of the neighbors."

It was a thirty minute drive. There was an old, rusted mailbox along the side of the road next to the driveway, but they could not see the house itself because it was obscured by a hill. May got out and opened the box but there was no mail inside. They drove an additional two miles before they found another driveway.

"Want to go see if anyone is home?" asks Holland.

"Might as well."

They approached a house which was visible from the road. It had a barn and a paddock with two horses. An older man was changing the oil on his tractor and met them as they approached.

"Good morning, folks, can I help you?"

May introduces herself, presents her badge and says with a friendly voice, "Good morning. We're making some inquiries about your neighbor to the east. What can you tell us about him?"

"Well, the owner lives in St. Paul, and he hasn't lived in the farmhouse for eight years. He rents it out from time to time. I'm leasing the land from him to grow hay and alfalfa for the horses."

"Is it rented out now?"

"A young man lives there. Looks like he could be Indian. He's been there for over a year, but I don't know much about him, I think he lives alone. I talked with him a few times when I work the field. He came by two days ago and asked if he could rent one of the horses, just for the day. We came to an arrangement. I offered him a saddle, but he said he preferred going native, thought that was kind of funny. He left his van here, hopped on the horse and rode off. He brought it back four hours later. Cannot tell you much else. What is this all about?"

"Just doing some follow up. Please keep this conversation private sir, and thanks for your assistance."

Back at the GAU they update Strouse who has called the team together. May has her tablet out and has highlighted the route on Google Earth. "The address where they delivered the equipment is on the same route as the one that we followed when we were tailing him. The farmhouse is eight miles further and half a mile east on a dirt road. There's a very good chance that he's still there."

Strouse asks about the veterinary supply store. "What did you find out from them?" Again, May speaks "They gave a positive ID but were reluctant to give up much when we asked what he purchased, but Holland here can be very persuasive when he gets hungry. He purchased things like chloroform, and a bunch of drugs to sedate animals during surgery. I have a list at my desk. He paid cash but some of the stuff was restricted to veterinarians, and he didn't show a license."

Strouse takes over and says, "Ok, we proceed on the assumption that he's still there. First, we need to confirm that he isn't out shopping or whatever. Second, we need to know if Linda Spalding is there. From the photos on Google Earth, we can see it will be difficult to set up surveillance since there's little to no traffic, and no other buildings except for the detached garage, it's wide open farmland. Check to see who the legal owner is. See if they know anything else about who he rented it to. Check with the utilities, who signed up for service and when. I'll get the search warrants and see if I can get a tap put on that phone number. We should at least be able to get a location and see if he's still making or receiving calls. The longer we wait the greater the danger there is to Linda. We'll slip in tonight and look for the van. If it's in the garage, we hold off until late morning and hope that he goes out. Then move in. If he hasn't left by noon, we go in. Check to see if the city has any permits for the house. If we're lucky, they may have some construction plans. Bring the thermal imaging camera.

May asks, "Do we invite SWAT?"

Strouse says, "That's up to Captain Jackson. For now, let's focus on getting as much information as we possibly can so we don't go in blind. Holland and I will go and set up on the road posing as DTE Energy maintenance workers. Get to work people."

Chapter 95

Linda snaps at him, "Stop asking me how I'm feeling! It hasn't gotten any easier over the last three days!"

"I'm sorry, it's almost finished, two, maybe three hours and it will be complete. I've put in a call to your photographer and he'll be here tomorrow. I'll go and get the horse in the morning. We'll release the pictures, video and documents right after your 'escape'. There is a Toyota Camry in the garage and the keys are by the back door. You can wear the clothing from the other girls, I have them upstairs. I'll call my lawyer one hour after you're gone. Where are you going to go? I suggest you call 911 from the nearest store or gas station and wait for the police to pick you up there. You had better hide the bag of money somewhere along the route because they will surely confiscate and search the car."

They had gotten along pretty well under the circumstances. She had made some suggestions about his art, but he had rejected them out of hand. He did like her idea of putting a steel collar around her neck or wrists with a chain representing how the natives were still enslaved.

Two hours later the work was completed. They went upstairs where there was a full length mirror. It was fantastic, covering her from the neck down to her hip. Somehow, he had even managed to present the horrific deaths of his sister and mother at the hands of those he felt responsible, in the same way as the crucifixion of Jesus Christ on the Cross. His sister is caught in the machine, a small boy sits on the ground pulling at one of her legs. The scene is heavy with tension, the sky brooding in swirling shades of deep crimson and smokey gray, as if nature itself recoils at the act unfolding below. At the center, his mother hangs from the rugged wooden beam, her frame taut with suffering, her eyes half-closed, with tears running down her cheeks. Shadows carve into her face, accentuating both anguish and the quiet acceptance of her fate.

Encircling them, are the employees of Treeman Oil and Gas like soldiers standing with hardened indifference, their tools catching the dim light of the setting sun. One raises a large wrench, glinting ominously, while the media rolls dice at her feet. High above, an FBI agent, his gun and badge prominently displayed watches with an unreadable expression—duty-bound yet perhaps shaken by the magnitude of what has been done. Mr. Treeman walks away holding a fist full of money. On the outskirts, the tribal chiefs observe with stern satisfaction, their robes pristine against the dust and sorrow of the moment, unmoved by the suffering that seals their decision. The entire composition is a stark contrast of power and sacrifice, casting a solemn weight upon the world that watches in silence.

If she wished, she could cover herself easily, but that was not his or her goal. She wanted the publicity as much as he did. She need it, craved it, like an addict craved their next fix. This would keep her in the spotlight for as long as the trial lasted, and that was usually measured in years.

Linda says, "I need a shower and then I'm going to bed, you may join me!"

He had been watching her while she admired his work. "Thanks for the offer, but I have a lot of work to do before the photographer arrives tomorrow. I need to setup the backdrops for the photo shoot."

She gives him a dismissive flip of the shoulders, turns and has thoughts that he might be gay. "I'll need hair and makeup essentials, as well as a hairdryer in the morning. Do you have them?"

There is a storm of silence behind her. She stops and turns back. "You've got to be kidding, your perfect plan and you didn't think of these? There's no way I am getting in front of the camera without proper hair and makeup."

Neither of them can risk going out in public at this point. No doubt the DPD has his picture distributed by now and she can't be spotted on a Walmart security camera when she is allegedly being held against her will.

She thinks for a moment, "Can you get Brett Rounders to pick up what I need? He certainly knows what a girl needs to get ready for a photoshoot."

"I'll text him. With what I'm paying him he shouldn't make a fuss about stopping at a store."

Chapter 96

It's noon on the fourth day of her imprisonment, and she is exhausted. She still feels the effect of ten thousand punctures, even though she has taken more Advil than she wanted. Brett has packed up and left. Mathew and she have been reviewing his work. The pictures are even better than they imagined. He was worth every penny. There are over one hundred and fifty pictures to scan and they need to pick out a dozen for the media and billboards. She'll keep the rest on a USB drive and distribute them slowly over the next few months. She has picked out one for her book cover. All of the pictures are based on the same theme, a beautiful native girl in a sexually seductive manner. Somehow Brett Rounders has skillfully positioned her so that the photos will pass censorship of the editors. The man was a genius with a camera.

She feels a bit guilty about how fortunate she is to benefit from her abduction. The other girls went through the same thing but received nothing.

She goes to the bathroom and washes the makeup off her face and messes up her hair. It's time to leave but it will all be in vain if they are caught before the package is distributed and the DPD confiscate it as evidence. She picks up her duffel bag and walks to the car without another word.

Chapter 97

May is on the phone as she waits for the city clerk to pull up construction permits when Styles taps her on the shoulder, "Just got a call from dispatch, someone claiming to be Linda Spalding called 911. Says she was kidnapped and just escaped. She's in a garage four miles from River's house. There's a unit on the way."

May hangs up the phone and grabs her jacket off the back of her chair and pulls the gun out of the desk drawer. "Let's go before the media hounds get to her. Tell the unit to go in without sirens. We don't want them to alert River in case he doesn't know that she has escaped. Strouse and Holland were on their way to the stakeout, did they see anything?"

"Haven't heard, they must have just missed her."

Holland is driving the DTE Energy van when Strouse's phone rings, it's T-Mobile. The cellphone just sent a call to a number assigned to a law firm.

May calls Strouse to tell him they're on their way to interview Linda Spalding. "I'm afraid he'll run if he finds out she's missing."

Strouse tells her about the call to the law firm. "Perhaps his intent is not to run. Maybe he plans to surrender with the aid of a lawyer."

Strouse thinks for a moment, it makes sense. River is after publicity, he wants to promote how the oil company, his tribe and everyone else has ignored what has happened. He has probably alerted the media so that they can film him on the news at six walking into the precinct with his lawyer. Making the DPD look stupid.

"This isn't going to play out the way he wants. Forget the interview, have the patrol unit pick her up and take her to the station or hospital if needed. You two come straight here. We are taking him before his lawyer gets there."

Ten minutes later they arrive at the entrance to the farm road. Strouse and Holland have already put on their vests. Styles and May retrieve theirs from the trunk. May shows surprise when Styles pulls out the Winchester Model 97. It's not standard issue for detectives, but she seems comfortable handling the big riot gun. She racks it to load a round.

The three group around Strouse, "SWAT is out on another call. Don't know how long they'll be because it's a hostage situation. We'll go in alone. So far, he hasn't given any indication that he's armed, but we aren't taking any chances, none, absolutely none. We're not taking a bullet for this piece of shit.

"Holland and Styles will drive the van straight in. May and I will drive the sedan right behind you. If he's watching we may be shielded from his view and give us a few seconds before he realizes this is a raid.

"Holland, Styles, you station yourselves on either side of the front door. We'll go to the side entrance and when we yell police, we all go in hard. If the door is locked, use the shotgun to open it. Once in we'll give him one chance to surrender. If he doesn't respond in five seconds we sweep the house. You take the front, we take the back. Meet at the stairs when the main level is clear. Then we'll decide if we go up or down. Any questions?"

There are none, they get into their vehicles, and Holland leads the way down the drive. Through the dusty windshield Holland sees the front door open. Mathew River steps out, he has removed his shirt. His arms are extended over his head. Styles had lowered the window on the way down the driveway, jumps out before the van is fully stopped. She lays the shotgun on the bottom of the window door frame. She screams at the top of her voice "on your knees, now." Holland takes a quick glance over to her, he has never heard that level of anger in her voice before. Visions of her father housed in a second rate facility cause her to blink. Had she not done everything possible to look after him? Had she made a mistake reporting the bribe?   Her finger slides from the trigger guard. He had done this to her, questioned her love for her father and tested her loyalty to the DPD and her fellow detectives.

May comes up behind her and gently lays a hand on her shoulder. "Looks like you got him." She relaxes and eases her finger off the trigger. May takes the shotgun and Styles is quick to put on the cuffs, a little tighter than normally required. "Tisk, tisk that, you should have called your lawyer earlier!"

It's all over in five minutes. He's put in the back seat of the sedan until a cruiser can take him in. The detectives search the house in case there's an accomplice and they look for evidence they can use during the trial.

May feels relief as the adrenaline high leaves her body. In some ways she's disappointed he didn't resist. She feels that a different outcome would make it easier for all the girls if they didn't have to testify or witness a long trial. They had already gone through so much.

Epilogue

May, Miles, Malinda and Diane sit in front of the TV watching the Tonight Show on NBC. Linda is being interviewed about her horrendous experience at the hands of her abductor. She is wearing, well, almost nothing. Jimmy Fallon is holding up the cover of her new book, not yet written.

Miles is grinning from ear to ear. Diane is sitting on the couch next to him, she gives him a look. He doesn't notice or perhaps doesn't care. She gives him a stiff elbow in the ribs. "Eyes back in your head boy."

"Who wants another drink?" Miles gets up to play bartender.

May says, "I doubt she has even written a word."

Malinda speaks up, "I heard that they have started jury selection. Maybe she wants to include the trial in the book. You can't open a magazine without seeing at least one picture of her. How many pictures did he take and who is distributing them?"

May's phone rings and she gets up to answer it. "Hello May, it's Brenda McDonald, have you got a second?"

"Hi Brenda, how are you? Sure, go ahead."

"I'm fine, I don't know if I should tell you this, but the other girls have talked about it. The thing is, we all received something in the mail and we don't know what to do with it. Some of us want to keep it, and someone else doesn't know if we should turn it in. We all trust you but are worried that if you knew, this would put you in an awkward position, so I don't know what to do."

May moves farther away from the group.

6644 "Well, tell me what it is that you got."

"We all got a shoe box."

"A shoe box?"

"Inside each box there was fifty thousand dollars, no note, no return address."

May thinks for a moment, turns to look at the TV and smiles. "Sounds like you have found someone that's willing to give you a little help."

The End

Echoes of the Past

Quiet breezes by me pass
Carrying whispers of the past
When magic and wisdom did abound
In everything as you looked around
Even now there is an echo in the air
Telling secrets to those who can hear
Only now it is a fading whisper
Twitching in silence like cat's whiskers

Slowly I am led on the course of the past
Where magic is seen everywhere
Where learning is the path to self-power
Nothing is learned within the hour
I have not left this life where I have grown
I have not traveled to places unknown
Yet I have time-traveled more than others know
Learning there what is fading now
Without the past we have no future

By Sylvyrwyng

HENK SLUIS

16783621R00187